A
MORE
ANCIENT
EVIL

A MORE ANCIENT EVIL

BOOK ONE

RYAN HOYT

To those who have fled from the confines of Raventree Hollow:
There is no true escape
They will find you

Te xi ce xi agalla exaltia
    Tsal ni alwen komoa niti
    Goa niti exselsien alwen tsal
    Tsalla bugga totia ni alwen komoa niti
    Tsalla como niti exselsien komoa fin

— TSALEXALTIA NEKROMANTIK
ENCHIRIDION; ANONYMOUS

A
MORE
ANCIENT
EVIL

PART
ONE

TSALEXALTIA
NEKROMANTIK
ENCHIRIDION

CHAPTER 1

SUNDAY, AUGUST 28, 1966

The cellar wasn't a cramped affair like one would imagine stepping into, entering down that lesser-used set of stairs behind the kitchen. Even calling it a cellar or basement was probably unfair to anyone on the receiving end of the story. It was larger than any house one could ever dream of owning, expanding the breadth of the manor under which it dwelt and even beyond, were one to consider the corridors jutting off at all sides.

The masonry in the underground behemoth was finer than any on the squat and ordinary buildings downtown. Arched ceilings gave the corridors the air of caves hidden away from the world, leading to treasures unimaginable in the depths of the earth, sans only the stalagmites and stalactites to really convince the out-of-place visitors they were in a natural cavern.

To the dismay of visitors, these offshoot tunnels were blocked off by velvet ropes hung from stanchions temporarily installed by the operators of the estate sale. There was one exception, a hallway that had been hastily boarded up at some point in recent history, the wood too fresh and the work too sloppy to be of the same material and craftsmanship as anything else in the estate. From the seams between each plank, a foul odor emitted, a hint of sulfur and rotten eggs, dying off as it mixed with the oxygen in the rest of the basement. It was just enough to send Wynette Strode jogging back toward the more populated chambers of the place.

"I was getting ready to assemble a search party for you in case you wandered down one of those blocked-off hallways," Wynette's irate mother said. The strands of white hairs that grew sporadically among the older woman's orange locks practically glowed from the occasional naked bulbs hanging just overhead, the only pinpricks of light in the place. "You'd think with the prices they've set on all this junk, they could afford to install some decent lighting. I seriously thought I'd lost you."

Wynette rolled her green eyes, knowing her mother wouldn't be able to see the gesture for the same reason she was complaining. She had to agree with her mother, though. How could anyone be expected to assess the condition of any items stored in the dark corners of this underworld? Perhaps the sellers had hoped to hide the rodent droppings and the moth-chewed fabrics of the discarded furniture down here, hoped that the visitors would be satisfied just to take anything out of the aristocrats' bourgeois mansion that overlooked their podunk little town. Wynette had no such illusions herself, not even being from around here.

Her mother had guilted her into taking this road trip, zigzagging through parts of the country she'd never seen—and that she wished she'd have kept that way now that she had seen it—on their way east to North Abbey, New York. Wynette was set to start her sophomore year in college in just two weeks. Two weeks that she *should* have been spending with Kevin, locked away in his house with no cares—and no clothes—since his parents were off gallivanting around Europe and their house was otherwise empty. Two weeks of pleasure, followed by a few hours on the plane back to the wretched East Coast to start another year with the stuck-up wenches she could barely tolerate but was forced to room with. She hadn't even wanted to join the sorority, but her mom had guilted her into that, too—"It'll help you build relationships that will last a lifetime," her mother had said —and it was the part about college she least wanted to return to. The girls all hated her, and the only reason she'd even been accepted was that, after a particularly brutal spell of initiation tests and hazing by the school's fraternities the previous year, Montague College's administrators had made a rule that during Rush Week nobody could be discriminated against.

"Would you look at this?" Wynette's mother asked, snapping her out of her dread. She looked around until she found her mother hunched over a rocking bassinet. "I wish you still played with your dolls. This would be perfect for one of the babies."

"God, Mom, I'm nineteen years old. Will you stop guilting me for finally trashing those things?"

Her mother rose up and morphed her face into an exaggerated frown. "You sure know how to break my heart. When you left home for your first year of college, you were still my little girl. What came home was a bitter woman, hell-bent on destroying all remnants of her childhood. I'd put the blame on that Calvin boy—"

"His name is Kevin," Wynette interrupted.

"—but he doesn't even go to college. No, I think your problem is that you aren't making friends at that school. I said you'd make the most of your experience if you joined a sorority, found like-minded gals, but you had to prove me wrong. You had to be antisocial and not participate in any of their activities or social gatherings."

"You're mad that I didn't come home a raging alcoholic like the rest of those girls?"

"Absolutely not, but it wouldn't hurt to let loose once in a while." Her mother walked toward a wall lined with bookshelves. Wynette remained next to the bassinet with arms crossed, attempting defiance despite her mother no longer paying her any mind. A draft blew through the cellar, carrying a hint of that stench she'd noted coming through the boarded-up corridor. The breeze caused the bassinet to rock, and Wynette flinched at the sight of it. She jogged after her mother.

The volume of lighting overhead had doubled where the bookshelves were, granting at least some ability to see the letters on the spines of the books. The shelves stretched about twenty feet to a corner, then another ten feet along the intersecting wall. Most of the segments of shelving were packed to the brim, though a few books leaned here or there over gaps where patrons had removed some ancient treasures during the sale. A gentleman that looked roughly her grandfather's age was stooped down just a few feet from her mother, flipping through the pages of a volume he'd discovered. Wynette's mother ran her finger along the spines on a shelf at eye level.

"Maybe we'll find something you can take with you to school and share with the other girls," Mrs. Strode said as she scanned the titles.

"Ah, going off to college, are you?" The old man's voice caused Wynette to jump. He laughed gently. "I'm so sorry. I did not mean to frighten you. I sent my sons off to college years ago and they rarely come back except the infrequent visit to dump the grandkids on my doorstep for a weekend. Quite the usual story in this town."

"Oh, we're not from here," Mrs. Strode said. "Just passing through on our way to Montague College in New York."

The man fumbled through his pockets and pulled out a handful of candies. "That's a long drive. How about a butterscotch for the road?" He held his hand out toward Wynette, but she just stood there with a grimace on her face. Her mother tapped her on the hip.

"Go on and take them," Mrs. Strode whispered. "Be polite for once in your life."

"Thank you," Wynette muttered as she reached for the hard candies. They were warm from his body heat, even slightly damp. She shoved them into the pocket of her jeans and forced a smile at the old man who still stared at her as if expecting her to eat the butterscotch right then and there.

His lips parted in a smile that would be goofy were it not for the brown rot that stained his teeth. "Those aren't just any drugstore penny candies, young lady. They're Wellworth's Fine Butterscotch, made right here at the confectionary in town. Finest butterscotch in the world, bar none. Don't forget to brush your teeth afterwards or yours will turn out like mine." He laughed at his own advice, then stooped down and gathered an armful of books. "These will do just fine to fill my shelves and make me look more cultured. Have a good trip, ladies."

With that, he was gone.

"Nice gentleman," Mrs. Strode said as she turned back to the shelves. She hummed for a minute before cutting off the tune with a squeal. She pulled out a book. "Oh, well this looks like a good time! Maybe a fun activity you can do with your sorority sisters."

She held the book out to Wynette, much like the old man and his butterscotch.

Wynette sighed and snatched the book from her mother. A shock ran through her as the pads of her fingers grazed the cover. She caught the faint tinkling of bells somewhere so distant it was nearly inaudible. The book felt both freezing cold and burning hot at the same time. It was both absurdly heavy and uncannily light. It reeked of must and mold, yet she did not find herself repulsed.

She took a step directly under a lightbulb and studied the book. Wynette had no doubt the tome was an antique, maybe even older than the house under which they stood. She ran her fingers along the cover, taking in the texture. It was uncanny. Not the expected feel of leather with its stickiness and light creases, but rather something more akin to reptile scales.

"Maybe it's snakeskin," her mother said, as if reading her mind. Wynette ignored her as she turned the book to read the spine. The characters were written in gold, though she could just barely make out the first word. *Tsalexaltia*? She wasn't positive, and wouldn't have been able to pronounce it either way. The second and third words were *Nekromantik Enchiridion*. A shiver rattled through her body as she flipped through the pages, her eyes taking in what appeared to be incantations and guides for some kind of rituals.

"You want me to take a book of witchcraft to college? Like that is going to make me popular with those prissy bitches?"

"Language, Wynnie, please. And yes, it's obviously just pretend. You know witchcraft isn't real. Have a good time with it! You can light candles and put on an album of spooky tunes. It will be such a blast."

Wynette shook her head and made to put the book back on the shelf, but something tugged at her heart. It wasn't guilt of offending her mother, but rather something deeper within, pleading her to keep the antique item. Like a piece of her soul yearning for the book.

"I..." she began, but found she didn't have any words. *I what?* she wondered as she pulled the book against her chest and hugged it much like she used to do with those very dolls her mother had chastised her for tossing in the garbage. "Okay, I'll take it. Thanks, Mom."

Wynette's school year hadn't started off as bad as the previous year. After two weeks in a car with her mother, she actually found herself excited to talk to anyone other than the woman she'd plopped out of nineteen years earlier. Back at the Lambda Psi Chi sorority house, she found a mutual respect with the returning girls, like veterans of a war sharing camaraderie amongst each other. Her ascension from freshman to sophomore seemed to help, not to mention the absence of the catty gals that had graduated at the end of last semester, allowing for a more genuine and intimate atmosphere in the house. The new frosh pledges were a down-to-earth bunch, and everyone just seemed to click so nicely together.

And there were fewer parties. This particular Friday night, for instance, ten of the girls remained at home despite the handmade flyers they had received inviting them to any of a dozen frat or sorority parties; the remaining six that lived in the sorority house during the week returned to their families in towns close enough to drive home to. Wynette was actually shocked at the unanimous decision among the ten of them to stay at home and just spend time together. Some blamed it on the uncharacteristically high October heat, others on burnout from a difficult first month of the semester, while others still just claimed to be too tired. Wynette certainly didn't feel sleepy or worn out from school, and she'd secretly been looking forward to a get together at the Gamma Rho Mu house—Gavin Anderle had personally invited her, and she had immediately forgotten Kevin's entire existence in that hunk's presence—but something pulled at her from deep within. It was like there was a magnetic force keeping all the girls tethered to their house.

Despite the collective adamance to stay home, however, the girls found themselves very bored very quickly.

"How about a board game?" Catherine Walton, one of the new recruits, suggested. She was sprawled out on one of the sofas, her legs over the lap of her best friend, Pam Yoshimoto. The couches and chairs in the social room had all been brought together in a circle, a common formation for the girls so far this semester. It allowed them to sit amongst each other as equals, chatting and taking turns telling stories about their days. There was just enough room for everyone, though some girls had to double up on the wider cushions. Wynette was one of the lucky ones, snagging one of the two recliners, even if it was a little heavier and more awkward to drag into the circle from its usual corner of the room.

"Like Monopoly?" Pam asked her friend.

"Boring. That game is more like *Snore*-opoly," Melinda McDonald, a senior, quipped. Even as pleasant as the sorority was this year, Melinda was the closest to retaining the previous year's less pleasant attitudes. She'd been a member for three years, so Wynette understood why the habit was hard to break, but she wished the older girl would try just a bit harder. The other seniors had had no problem adapting to the newer, friendlier demeanor the sorority had shifted to. "I think I *will* go out to Greek Row and find some boys to dance with."

"Wait," Marnie Redmond pleaded. Marnie was Wynette's roommate for the second year in a row and the closest thing to an actual friend she had at the college. Marnie turned to Wynette and flashed what resembled a brief apology before turning back toward Melinda. "Wynnie has a book we can grab and—"

"Read stories together like a bunch of dweebs?" Melinda interrupted.

"—conjure up some spirits!" Marnie continued, not deterred by Melinda's snark.

"Like one of those Ouija boards?" Pam asked. "My grandmother said those are not to be messed with."

"They're made by a toy company, Pam. How dangerous can they be?" Catherine asked.

"It's all just the power of imagination," Kristina Woodrow chimed in. "The planchette only moves because people subconsciously will it to. No ghosts involved."

"This is something different," Marnie said. "Like an ancient spell book or whatever."

"I never showed that to you. Were you going through my things?" Wynette asked. She was certain she'd left the book in one of her suitcases tucked in the back of the closet, too embarrassed to bring it out for this exact reason. So much for having a good year and being respected by her sorority sisters.

"Sorry," Marnie said. She sounded sincere enough that Wynette softened her glare. "I was looking for that checkered skirt you bought last year and couldn't find it in your drawers. I wanted to borrow it for my scene in drama class last week. It would have looked perfect! When I opened the suitcase and noticed that old book, I just had to reach in and grab it. It's like no book I've ever seen before. I swear it holds some kind of power."

"Okay, I have to see this," Melinda said. Wynette caught a sneer on the senior's face. It wasn't the book she was interested in at all, just Wynette's discomfort. "Go fetch it, Marnie."

Marnie didn't look back to Wynette for permission. She jumped up, left the circle, and darted up the stairs to their room.

"I'll grab the candles," Hannah Rigby offered, following Marnie to the second floor.

"I can't believe we're doing this," Pam said and went on about her grandmother's warnings. "The occult is no joke," she concluded as someone tossed a decorative pillow at the side of her head.

"Let's go, ladies," Hannah said as she returned with candles tucked under both arms. "Someone open the basement door for me."

"Basement?" Pam yelped. "Why do we need to go down there?"

"It's either that or the attic," Greta Heyerdahl said, "and the attic is probably a hundred degrees right now. The basement will have all the right vibes, guaranteed. Come on!"

The girls followed, even Wynette, despite her feeling of betrayal from her roommate. As she passed the stairs on the way toward the kitchen, Marnie descended with the antique tome clutched tightly against her chest. Wynette's knees buckled and a wave of nausea crashed over her.

Marnie lunged down the last two steps and reached out with an arm to steady her. "You okay, Wynnie?"

Wynette nodded, but her eyes were locked on the book under Marnie's left arm. She was suddenly not so sure that she was okay.

Perhaps they should have gone out that Friday night after all.

CHAPTER 3

"I can't believe we're doing this," Pam said as the girls gathered in the dimly lit basement. Hannah and her best friend Haley Crockett were lighting the candles and setting them in the approximation of a circle that had been hastily drawn in chalk by Allie Forsyth.

"It'll be *so* much more fun than Monopoly, Pammie," Catherine said in a sarcastic tone unlike the girl's usual sweet nature. Wynette knew she was only trying to appeal to Melinda. Wynette had known several girls like Catherine over the years. She thought of them as *chameleons*, changing who they are to adapt, not caring which friends they hurt in the process. In just over a year, Wynette had met too many chameleons. She'd give it just another couple weeks before the girl alienated the friendship of her roommate Pamela to impress the snarky Melinda. Catherine seemed to sense her judgment; she turned her eyes to Wynette and furrowed her brow before continuing to speak to Pam. "It's not a big deal. Just lighten up and try to have fun."

Marnie jabbed her elbow into Wynette's arm. She turned to her roommate and couldn't help the look of disappointment she flashed. She reminded herself of her mother. "What?" she whispered. Marnie held the book out as a peace offering.

"It's your book. Flip through the pages to whatever you want us to try, and we'll do it. Your choice." Marnie's eyes held no malice, and despite her best attempt, Wynette found she couldn't hate the girl. She accepted the book and stepped over to one of the cones of light shining down from the ceiling. It dawned on her in that moment that she had been in a cellar when her mother found the book, and now she was in another when the book would be put to use.

Maybe I'll die *in a cellar, too,* she thought and chuckled softly.

Not softly enough, apparently.

"Strode is *so* into this," Melinda goaded from across the room. "The girl's been with us a year and we had no idea she's actually a witch. You learn something new every day."

"Yeah, who would have thought Wynette of all people would be Satan's little helper," Catherine added, looking at Melinda for approval.

Wynette ignored them and flipped through the pages for the first time since that dark basement where her mother had found the antique item. The pit in her stomach grew as she got deeper into the book, her eyes soaking up the unusual and grotesque imagery on each page. There were illustrations of flayed men, closeups of genitalia that made her blush, severed pieces of animals, and creatures that looked straight out of those Lovecraft books her boyfriend Kevin loved to read. Why had her mother insisted she buy this disgusting artifact? It was certainly something a young woman would have been tortured and executed for possessing hundreds of years ago in Salem, not a social night centerpiece or a form of entertainment for a group of precocious sorority gals.

"That's a creepy one," Melinda said, having moved across the room to get a closer look at the pages Wynette thumbed through. She grabbed the book out of Wynette's grasp and held it closer to the light hanging above. "Like some sort of tentacles or something. Maybe one of them will pop out between my legs after our little séance and I can be more hung than Gary Haberman from Epsilon Iota Pi. He'll lose his status as *big man on campus* after that."

Most of the girls cracked up at that, all except Wynette and Pam. Even Marnie thought it was a riot, though when her eyes caught Wynette's, she tried her best to straighten her face.

It was at that point when Melinda started reading off the page. The words coming out of her mouth were unrecognizable. She paused and looked around at the girls. "It looks like it's written in English characters, but it reads like a bunch of nonsense."

"Latin?" Pam asked, her voice barely a squeak.

"Oh I know Latin," Melinda said. "I'm a lapsed

Catholic, remember? This is most definitely *not* Latin. Can someone turn out those lights?"

Hannah complied, having just completed setting the last of the candles around the circle's perimeter with Haley. She rushed to the foot of the stairs and flipped the switch. The room fell into near darkness, the candles barely illuminating the space. Wynette's breath caught. She felt like a weight was crushing her chest. She lost her balance and stumbled, kicking a candle and knocking it over.

"Don't burn the place down, Strode," Melinda taunted. "Come on, girls. Everyone sit in the circle. There's room for all of us—just suck it in a little, Greta."

Marnie grabbed Wynette's elbow and helped her gently to the floor. The other girls followed suit, plopping down onto their bottoms, their legs crossed in front of them like pretzels.

"Deep breaths," Marnie whispered. Wynette complied, getting her sudden panic attack under control while the other girls looked on uneasily. Marnie addressed them on Wynnie's behalf. "She's okay. She's not a big fan of enclosed spaces. Go on, Melinda."

The de facto leader rolled her eyes at this but went on reading in the unknown language on the page. With every strange word the senior said, Wynette felt the room getting colder and colder and colder. She let out a breath in a sound of shock and was even more surprised to see the steam emitting from her mouth as if she were outside on a crisp winter morning. It was ninety degrees that day. There was no way the temperature could have dropped so drastically, even in a dark cellar.

"What the hell?" she muttered to herself, but even Marnie didn't seem to hear it. The girls were all too entranced by whatever Melinda was reading out of the book.

CHAPTER 4

"Tuh... chee... say... chia... galla... ex... exaltia?" Melinda plopped the book down on her lap and shook her head.

"You're doing so good," Catherine said. Out of the corner of her vision, Wynette saw Pam's jaw drop at her roommate's brown-nosing. Oblivious, Catherine went on. "Maybe we should all hold hands and make it a continuous circle. I think I've seen that in a movie about witches."

Melinda chuckled at that. "Right, and then maybe we should take all our clothes off and spin in a circle together. Was that something they did in your little movie?"

"No, but I'm game for it if you think it will help, Melinda." There was no insincerity in the poor freshman's voice. *That's a girl that will meet her demise in a death cult one day*, Wynette thought. Without meaning to, she giggled. Everyone turned to stare at her, but it was Melinda's glare that burned into her most.

"Spill it, Strode. You think you can do this better than me? It is your book after all."

Wynette shook her head vigorously. "No, I really don't. I agree with Catherine that you're doing great." She was disappointed in herself for her cowardice. Something inside her begged for her to stand up, break the circle, and leave. Walk up the stairs and right out the front door. Whatever was happening here was not going to end well. The more rational—or perhaps more cowardly—side of her had control, keeping her bottom glued to the frigid cellar floor. "Please, keep going."

"Let us at least repeat after you," Allie offered. She took the hands of the girls on either side of her as Catherine had suggested, and the others followed suit. Melinda was the only exception. She stood up in the center of the circle, causing the other girls to shift positions to make up for the new gap. Melinda bent for a candle to see the text before hoisting the book close to her face. She cleared her throat and went on.

"Tsal ni alwen komoa niti," she read with more confidence.

"Tsal ni alwen komoa niti," the other young women repeated in unison.

"Goa niti exselsien alwen tsal."

As they repeated the next line, four candles along the chalk line of the circle extinguished, causing the room to dim even further.

"Jesus, Greta, did you pass gas again?" Melinda accused. Wynette watched as Greta flinched from the harshness.

"That wasn't me," Greta said, as if the rude question even deserved a reply.

"I thought I felt something," Pam said in a high, nervous voice. "It was like a cold breeze."

"I didn't feel a thing, Pamela," Catherine said with a pitying tone. "Perhaps this is too much for you to handle. Do you want Wynnie to take you upstairs and the two of you can play a game of Tiddlywinks instead?"

Melinda whistled to recapture their attention. "Let's just keep reading. Tsalla bug... bugga totia ni alwen komoa niti." The girls attempted to repeat, though the words were pronounced in any number of ways. "Tsalla exaltia totia komoa niti." This time they were closer to her pronunciations, getting the hang of some of the repeated sounds. "Tsalla como niti exselsien komoa—"

Whoosh.

The wind was undeniable this time. Despite her hair being pulled back tightly in a ponytail, Wynette felt some of the missed strands in the front blow upward, then down into her face. The candles flickered and most went out. She looked around the circle and only counted three candles that still had a flame.

"Well that's sure dark," Kristina said, the fear as palpable in her voice as it was in Pam's moments earlier. Greta released her hold on her neighbors' hands, causing the rest of them to break the circle in succession.

Hannah rose and struck a match. "Do you still have your matches, Haley? Help me get these going again." She bent down and touched the lit match to the nearest candle's wick while Haley followed suit and attempted to light a different one.

"Weird," Haley said.

"Yours isn't taking to the flame either?"

Haley shook her head. "No. Are these cheap candles or something? Use them once and then throw them away?"

"Mickey brought them over last weekend when we… never mind. They worked fine both times I've tried to light them before."

A few of the girls shifted nervously around the circle. Wynette did her best to keep calm, but her heart didn't get the memo. She could feel it beating harder and faster in her chest. Racing. Thudding. Trying to break free, to rip itself out, protrude from her insides and explode all over her sorority sisters. She wasn't sure when she began shaking, but Marnie noticed and squeezed her hand.

"Hey," her roommate whispered. "It's okay, Wynnie. We're all fine. Calm down. Deep breaths, remember?"

"Oh come on, you babies," Melinda said. "Let's just keep reading and—"

Thump.

Thump.

Thump.

Melinda thought it was her heart for a moment before she realized the cadence was too slow.

"Are those…" Kristina started before trailing off at another succession

Thump.

Thump.

Creak.

Thump.

Closer. Closer.

"The floorboards," Pam said. "The creaky spot in the dining room. Someone's in the house."

A collective gasp came from throughout the circle as the girls recalled exactly the spot that bowed and made noise when walked over. They each crossed it daily on their way through the first floor of the house. The dining room was like a central artery, leading to the stairwell, the kitchen, the social room, the study.

"Was the front door locked?" Wynette asked.

"I always lock it," Hannah said. "You guys know it's a habit of mine from growing up in New York City."

"I came through the back door after taking out the trash earlier," Haley added. "I know I locked that one as well."

Creak.

Thump.

Thump.

Thump.

Thump.

The steps moved farther away.

"Okay, the only one of us with steps that heavy is Greta, and she's sitting right here," Melinda said. "So which one of you bitches wants to admit to making a copy of the key for your little boyfriends, huh? Hannah, maybe?"

"No, I swear."

"Me neither," Greta said. Her boyfriend Billy was over more than any other guy, but Wynette couldn't recall him ever letting himself in. It was a blatant violation of the house rules, and Greta was almost as much a stickler as Pam and Wynette herself.

"Fine," Melinda said, "I'm going to go up there and find out who it is. All this witchcraft crap is putting me in the mood anyways, so I can't promise I won't jump the bones of whoever he is."

She stepped through an opening in the circle of girls, kicking over two extinguished candles as she walked away and was lost in the shadows of the nearly dark basement.

"Can you hit the light switch on your way up?" Pam pleaded. They listened as Melinda ascended the stairs. The click of the light switch sounded out, but the bulbs didn't illuminate.

"What the hell?" they heard Melinda whisper. The switch clicked a few more times as she flipped it in rapid successions, but nothing happened. "Power is out or something," she called back. The knob turned. The door into the kitchen creaked open and slammed shut.

Breaths held, the girls listened as Melinda's feet pattered across the linoleum floor of the kitchen, growing distant.

A ticking sound commenced nearby. Rapid and repeating. Wynette squinted in the darkness and looked around at the other girls before stopping on Marnie. The girl's teeth were chattering. Her arms were crossed tightly.

"It's so cold," she whimpered to Wynette. "Don't... don't you feel it?"

Attempting to be as comforting to Marnie as

Marnie had been to her, Wynette reached over to rub her roommate's shoulder. The chill of the girl's skin caused her to flinch at the touch.

"Marnie, it's not that cold. You must be catching a—"

Whoosh.

"Cold," Catherine cried out as a gale wind tore through the basement. It was much more than a light breeze from a slammed door. Instinctively, all of the girls moved toward the center of the circle, shoulder to shoulder.

"Did someone leave a window open?" Kristina asked.

"They boarded them up last year after one leaked over winter break," Hannah recalled. "They don't open anymore. There's no opening except the door to the kitchen."

"Then what is—"

"Hello?" Melinda's muffled voice called out, causing Kristina to stop mid-sentence. "Whoever is in here, I'm going to clock you over the head with this very sturdy vase in my hands. Show yourself and it won't come to that."

The girls listened to the light patter of Melinda's footsteps as she moved into the social room. Wynette could picture the route around the circle of couches that Melinda must have taken.

"Wait, which way did the guy's footsteps go after he was above us?" Allie asked.

"Back toward the front door, I think," Greta said.

"No, he definitely went toward the stairs," Pam

whimpered. "He's probably up in one of the bedrooms now."

Thump.

Thump.

Thump.

The heavy footsteps were back. Greta was right. They were coming from somewhere near the front of the house.

Pat.

Pat.

Pat.

Melinda's lighter footsteps sounded out from the farthest corner of the social room as she made her way around the couches and back toward the dining room.

Thud.

Thud.

Pat.

Pat.

From opposite directions they came, but Wynette had no doubt they were converging right at the—

Creak.

CHAPTER 5

S ilence.

No heavy, thudding steps of a man in work boots.

No light patter of a young woman in house slippers.

Both paths had ended at the bowing floorboard directly over the pack of girls cowering together in the center of a chalked circle in the blackest darkness of the cellar.

The girls didn't dare speak. As far as Wynette could tell, they weren't even breathing, every girl as still and silent as possible, whether to ensure they heard any little sound from upstairs, or to remain hidden from whoever the intruder was up there.

Wynette cocked her head to the right as if that could help her hear a noise that wasn't there. Her eyes met Marnie's. The fear displayed on her roommate's face caused her to recognize her own. The two girls put their foreheads together and wrapped their arms around each other. Marnie wept first. Someone followed, perhaps Greta or Pam.

"Shhh," Wynette attempted, not wanting anyone to begin crying aloud and calling attention to their whereabouts. She feared the hushing would make it worse for her sisters, but they cut off their cries immediately.

Silence.

Drip.

Drip.

Wynette pushed herself away from Marnie and looked down. In the center of the circle, just between all of the girls, drops of liquid plopped down in rapid succession. She looked up. Condensation covered a circle on the ceiling.

The sprinkles turned into a gush as liquid poured down. The girls cried out or screamed as they dove out of the circle in every direction.

"What the hell is that?" Catherine asked.

"Melinda said something about hitting the guy with a vase," Marnie said. "Maybe she lifted it and water came out."

"That's a lot more water than a vase could hold," Hannah added.

"Was it blood?" Pam asked between sobs. "Is she dead?"

Wynette felt the liquid soaking into her arm. She brought her sweater sleeve up to her nose and sniffed. "It sure doesn't smell like blood to me." She held her arm out toward Greta, who was closest to her in that moment.

Greta gagged. "Oh God, it smells like pee," she managed between retches.

"You mean Melinda pissed herself? That poor girl!" Catherine cried. "We have to help her!"

"Are you kidding?" This from Pam. "We can't go up there. We'll die."

The girls all thought this was an intruder—a living, human intruder—but Wynette was not so certain. If the pictures in the book were to be believed, this was something else entirely. A wave of emotions washed over her. Fear. Confusion. Guilt weighed on her more than both of those. The book had been hers. She could have said no when Marnie mentioned it. She should have been adamant about not bringing it out. Had she not been part of the sorority this year, none of the girls would be in this situation. She had to swallow all of those feelings down and feign a different one. Bravery.

"We can do it. There are nine of us. Ten if Melinda is okay. I'm pretty sure there is only one intruder up there."

"What if he has a gun?" Hannah asked.

Wynette turned and headed toward the stairs before answering. "He can only shoot at one of us at a time while the others tackle him. Let's go."

She took the first few steps before the thought hit her that she was utterly alone, that the other girls hadn't followed her. By the time she reached the top of the staircase, however, she was glad to know she was wrong. Her sisters were all there just behind her, ready to rescue one of their own and drive a creep from their home.

She reached for the knob. It jiggled as her hands trembled, but she managed to wrap her fingers around it. She turned it a fraction of an inch.

Click.

CHAPTER 6

Wynette had no idea where the bravery came from. She'd always been too soft-spoken, too quick to cry when teased, too easily intimidated by anyone challenging her in the slightest. Yet there she was, mustering courage and leading the girls upstairs to their very potential deaths. As she reached the top step, she thought perhaps her newfound strength was born of the guilt she felt for ever having brought that wretched book into the sorority house.

I can deal with the blame later, she thought as she reached for the doorknob, *but for now we have a sister to save.*

When the knob met resistance, however, all courage dissipated.

"It's locked," she said. The parade of footsteps coming up the stairs halted in unison as her words registered with the other girls.

"Locked?" Marnie asked. "Whatever do you mean?"

"Maybe it's just stuck," Catherine offered. "Melinda would never lock us in the cellar."

"Unless this was all just some big practical joke," Pam said. "Wynnie, did you plan this with Melinda? It's a sick prank if so. You two should be ashamed of yourselves."

Wynette turned around from the top step and looked over the girls' faces. In the shadows, she couldn't make out the fear or the anger or the suspicion that each of them may have worn, so she knew she had to sound as sincere as possible so her own emotions and honesty would be clear. The last thing she needed was everyone turning against her in such a situation.

"I had absolutely nothing to do with this, other than regrettably bringing that book into this house. I'm so sorry, girls. Truly."

"It was my fault for suggesting we do this," Marnie said.

"You can say that again," Greta chimed in with an accusatory tone. "Move out of the way so I can try the door."

Wynette heard the shuffling of feet as the gals on the higher steps scooted against the railing to allow Greta to pass. She shoulder-checked Wynette at the top step, causing Wynette to lose her grip on the doorknob. She heard the jiggling of the handle and the soft swearing under Greta's breath.

"She's right," Greta said. "The bitch locked us in here. I never trusted Melinda, that good-for-nothing wench."

A gasp came from Pam, which quickly turned into

sobs. Catherine descended two steps and pulled her roommate into a hug.

"Shhh, it's okay, Pammie. Melinda would never do that to us. She—"

Clack.

Clack.

Clack.

Footsteps, though not of the same quality they'd previously heard from what Wynette thought of as the intruder's heavy boots, nor the padded sound of Melinda in her slippers. The steps sounded somewhat closer, too.

Is this a second intruder? Are they walking through the kitchen toward the cellar door? It didn't sound like it was coming from the kitchen, Wynette thought.

She backed down a step to the stair Catherine had just vacated. Greta did the same, and both girls cocked their heads to listen.

Silence.

The girls all fell into a hush, holding their breaths to listen in anticipation.

Another *clack* followed, and the faint sound of something light being knocked over. The tiny bit of light that had been left from the three remaining candles in the basement extinguished. It was pitch black.

"Those steps were *in* the basement," Greta half whispered, half cried. Several of the girls yelped in unison as they all darted toward the top of the stairs.

Wynette reached around Greta, grabbed the knob, and gave it a firm twist. This time it turned all the way just as the rush of her sisters reached the top. They pushed against Wynette and Greta. The door flew open and both girls at the top slammed down onto the linoleum floor of the kitchen at the landing while the others clambered over them. Someone came down hard on Wynette's hair and she screamed, which caused the other girls to panic even worse, unsure if someone was being attacked.

Once the others were through the doorway and into the kitchen, Wynette jumped to her feet and slammed the basement door. She twisted the deadbolt to the locked position and leaned with her ear against the door. She couldn't hear anyone coming up the stairs in pursuit.

Kristina tried the lights in the kitchen, but the switches just clicked with no result. Hannah whimpered. The breaths of some of the other girls picked up rapidly, as if they were starting to hyperventilate in unison.

"There's a flashlight under the kitchen sink," Haley recalled. There was just enough light coming in the window from the moon outside and the neighboring houses that Wynette could see her crossing the kitchen and crouching down to open the cabinet. Behind bottles of cleaning products and detergent, the junior located the silver flashlight that they kept in case of emergency. "Found it," she said as she thumbed the power switch.

It made a small ticking sound. The light pierced the darkness...

...And then faded to black, along with their hopes.

CHAPTER 7

"The lighter," Wynette called, her voice frantic. "There is one in the drawer with the birthday candles and cake decorations."

"I got it," Marnie said. She turned and opened a drawer just to the left of the oven. She rustled through all of the miscellaneous junk the girls kept in there. "Found it!"

A spark emitted as Marnie spun the wheel on the top of the lighter, but it snuffed out just as quickly. All the girls held their breaths and listened as Marnie's thumb rubbed along the wheel over and over again, but it was all for naught.

"I think there was a pack of matches in there too," Pam offered. "I remember using them for the candles on Haley's cake."

"It's no use," Wynette said. She didn't know why she was so sure, but deep inside she understood that whatever afflicted their house that night was forcing them to remain in pure darkness. "We all know our way around the house. Let's partner up and check every room."

The girls stood in silence as if they hadn't heard her. Or, more likely, as if they wished they hadn't. They were terrified just as she was, but it didn't matter. Their sister was missing, likely in some kind of trouble. They had to find her. She clapped her hands together twice, sending a few girls jumping.

"Right now, damn it!"

With that, the girls buddied up, Catherine with Pam, Hannah with Haley, Greta with Allie, Kristina with Marnie. That left Wynette on her own. She didn't quite mind. It meant she could run away at the sound of those heavy footsteps and not have to worry about leaving a partner behind.

While the other girls headed out of the kitchen, Wynette turned and walked back toward the door to the cellar stairs. It was still bolted; not that she doubted it would be, but she wanted to make sure. She put her ear to the door. There was no way someone else could have been down there with them. The noises they had heard just before the door opened must have been the remaining candles falling into the puddle of whatever had dripped down from the ceiling. Maybe rats jumping out after the girls had vacated the cursed circle. She tried to listen beyond the pounding of her terrified heart. Was that... *breathing?*

It couldn't be, and yet...

Silence.

Wynette pushed herself off the door. At a ninety-degree angle from the cellar door was the pantry. She pulled open the curtains that separated the alcove from the rest of the kitchen. It was large enough for three or four people to hide if they were huddled together, but it was empty besides the boxes of cereals, sacks of flour and rice, and bags of potato chips on the shelves. She moved back and pivoted to her left. She stepped through the doorway into the laundry room. A pile of towels took up the center of the room, just large enough to cover one body in fetal position, lying in wait.

The topmost rag slid off as she stared at it.

Something pulsed within.

"Melinda?" she whispered, but there was no reply. No more movement.

I'm imagining things, she thought.

Wynette reached out and grabbed onto the washing machine with her right hand for balance, then used her left foot to kick aside a layer of towels. The rest of the pile toppled over. No body underneath, alive or dead.

A creak in the kitchen caused her to turn back. Nobody was out there that she could see. Had it come from the basement stairs instead? Wynette wasn't sure, but she didn't want to wait around to find out. She walked through the kitchen and checked the back door. It was locked just as they had all thought.

She walked out of the kitchen, passing by the stair-well. She couldn't see any of the girls up on the stairs or the second-floor landing. She continued on into the dining room, where Hannah and Haley were peeking under the tablecloth in case Melinda had crawled under it to hide. She looked down at the floor, recalling the liquid that had dripped down, but the scratched-up hardwood looked completely dry.

"Did one of you wipe up any mess here?" she asked, her voice startling Hannah and causing the junior to slam her head on the bottom of the table.

"Damn it!" Hannah cried out.

"No, there was nothing on the floor. Maybe it was a burst pipe," Haley suggested. Wynette thought about it, but she could not recall any pipes over that part of the basement. She didn't want to worry the other girls by disagreeing, so she left it at that.

She stepped into the social room, where Catherine and Pam were tossing cushions off of the couches. Marnie stood near the piano consoling a weeping Kristina. With that room covered, Wynette passed through the dining room again and into the front room that was used as the study. Greta and Allie had just finished pulling all of the chairs away from the desks, but Melinda hadn't been found under any of them.

"Did you check the front door?" Wynette asked.

"Locked," Greta answered.

"Deadbolt and chain, too," Allie added.

Wynette nodded but walked through the room to the front door anyways. As they'd insisted, it was triple locked. She opened the coat closet door, the familiar smell of old jackets and shoes wafting out at her. She reached in and pushed at the coats, but neither Melinda nor the intruder were hiding in there.

"Upstairs, then," Wynette said as she walked past Allie and Greta, then Haley and Hannah. "Come on, girls."

Wynette stopped at the first step and looked up. She could make out the area just near the top of the second-floor landing, still looking as clear as it had a minute ago. She squinted higher toward the third floor, but there was no visibility that high. Taking a deep breath, she stood tall and began the climb.

At the landing, she pointed to the right and nodded toward Allie and Greta.

"Go that way. Haley and Hannah, check the rooms to the left. I'll go to the third floor. Send the others my way if they come up."

Wynette climbed to the third floor alone. If the intruder was up there and Wynnie screamed for help, how long would it take her housemates to come to her aid? She hoped she would not have to find out.

With the unbearable early October heatwave they'd been enduring, the third floor had been a miserable place to sleep. Some of the girls had been taking their blankets and pillows down to the social room and sleeping on the couches each night. Thus, Wynette was surprised to find with each step she ascended that it grew more and more frigid. There was a distinct odor she noted as she reached the top landing. It was earthy and damp at the forefront, but sniffing deeper, there was something else. A dying rodent. Sulfuric. Rotten eggs? It was something she'd smelled before, surely.

It hit her.

The cellar of that mansion where Mom found the book.

Perhaps that had been the last time she had felt such fear and uncertainty, and her brain was playing tricks on her, convincing her she smelled something that wasn't there.

Creak.

Wynette turned to see Marnie making her way up. In the slight amount of twilight coming through the windows of the surrounding rooms, she could make out her roommate's crinkled nose.

"You smell that?" Wynette asked.

"Does a ginger have freckles?" Marnie asked. It was a weird saying she had, which was even slightly offensive considering Wynette was as redheaded and freckled as they come. "It's like something croaked up here!"

"Hopefully not Melinda," Kristina whimpered as she came up behind Marnie.

Drip.

Drip.

Wynette met Marnie's hazel eyes in a stare of terror. "Maybe she wanted to take a bath?" Wynette offered. "I'll go check it out. You two check the rooms."

Wynette turned and headed down the hall toward the bathroom on the far end. She was certain they would have heard the bathwater running if Melinda had gone up to fill the tub. But, maybe they'd been too preoccupied with their fears to notice. Maybe Melinda had had an accident in the dining room, mopped it up with a towel or her dress, then ran up the stairs to bathe before the other girls could find out she'd peed herself in fear.

That had to be it.

Drip.

The door was only open a few inches, but its path

swung inward with the tub behind it. She'd have to go all the way inside and look behind the door to see if Melinda was in there.

"Mel? Can I come in? We're all worried about you," Wynette said gently. No answer. "Mel, it's Wynnie. I just want to check on you."

Silence.

Wynette pushed the door open further and stepped in. She turned toward the tub and gasped.

CHAPTER 8

Melinda was not in the bathtub, but it wasn't empty. It was at about half capacity, the water polluted with a cloudy pink from what looked like drops of blood throughout. Instead of mixing in and turning the water red, they stayed as individual blobs. The bathroom was partially illuminated by the moonlight, and Wynette could just make out blobs swimming around or wriggling their way through the water, maybe tearing themselves up as they traveled, bleeding out more.

Thwuck.

A sticky suckling sound came from the tub, followed by the formation of a whirlpool as the drain opened itself and the water made its way down into the pipes. The little bloody swimmers were pulled toward their doom, circling, massing together, yet Wynette thought they were fighting their demise as best they could.

Glug glug glug.

And then they were gone. The water went down,

leaving a pink ring where the waterline had topped out, and chunky residue like endometrial clots dotted the bottom of the tub. The drain made a gurgling sound. Wynette leaned over, but it was too dark to see inside the drain.

The tub vibrated. The entire room rattled. She braced herself, putting one hand to her right against the wall and the other across the tub against the white tile. She looked down at the drain and could just make out little pink bubbles, growing, multiplying. Getting larger, larger, ready to pop...

Splat.

As the mass of bubbles popped in unison, liquid and debris sprayed up into Wynette's face. She pushed off the wall, careful not to open her mouth and scream lest she suck the filth into her mouth. She wiped her hands across her face, her fingers tangling in whatever had stuck to her. She pulled her hands away to find them covered in bloody clumps of hair, slimy with the rot and decay from the drain. She flicked it all off toward the tub and ran across the bathroom to the sink, where she scrubbed her hands and face with soap and washed the filth away.

Soap got into her eyes as she scoured her face. She gasped at the unexpected sting and forced water into her eyes.

With the soap washed out, she squeezed her eyes shut as she searched for a towel. She reached over to where the hand towel should be, but her fingers met an empty rack. *Hannah is always taking the hand towel and not replacing it with a fresh one,* she thought, a petty thing perhaps, but a recurring annoyance nonetheless. Eyes still closed, she pivoted toward the wall to her left where a rack usually held two bath towels. At first swipe, she didn't feel anything. She swung her hand again.

Slap.

Her hand met skin. Warm. Sweaty. She pulled her arm in quickly and forced her eyes open. Her vision was blurry, the moisture obscuring her vision, but she was certain Melinda was standing in front of her, fully naked.

"Mel," Wynette gasped.

She brought her right arm up and wiped her eyes in the crook of her elbow, improving her vision. She blinked. Melinda was not standing there at all. The bathroom was just as empty as it had been.

I'm losing it, she thought.

Whatever had happened to the bathtub, they could look at it later and give it a good scrubbing. The plumbing in this old house had always been terrible, so maybe with all the women living here, their loose hairs had finally done a number on the old pipes and clogged them. The blood could have been menstrual blood from one of the girls, or it may have just been a trick of the shadows. That had to be it. Right now, her housemate was missing. She had to press on and find Melinda. She took a step toward the doorway.

The door swung closed, smacking Wynette's left temple and knocking her down to the tile floor. The world went black.

CHAPTER 9

Visions of a world surrounded by a thick, mucky fog rushed into Wynette's mind, replacing the pitch blackness that had overtaken her. She rolled from her back to her right side, curling into a fetal position. The squishy sound of thick, gooey mud sounded out. The smell of rot infested her nostrils, launching her into a gagging fit, each little movement squeezing more of the odor out of the muck in which she lay.

A pained squeal pierced the thick air, taking on a warbling quality as the sound waves distorted through the fog from some far-off distance. Pale greenish-gray light glowed through the clouds of filth. As much as she wanted to just close her eyes and wake up in the real world in her bed, putting this whole nightmare experience behind her, Wynette knew she had to move. She pushed off the ground with her right hand, but her palm slipped in the mud. More disgusting noises, more stench wafting up. Her right cheek slapped into the ground. She took a deep breath and tried again, this time successfully sitting up on her bottom, the moisture seeping through her pants.

Too light-headed to stand, she remained on her bottom and put one hand to each side of her for balance. The world spun around her. Her head ached from the door slamming into her, or from hitting the tile floor of the bathroom. A concussion perhaps? *Something* was responsible for this delusion anyways. There was no way this place was real.

Something crawled over her foot, tickling her in a most unpleasant way. That was enough to launch her up to her feet and push through the nausea. She kicked off whatever little critter was on the top of her foot and stepped backward, sliding a bit but keeping herself upright. The squeal sounded out again, this time much closer than before. This was the dominion of some unearthly creature, and she was trespassing.

A warm, wet wind blew from behind. Wynette turned to see the fog parting. Swarms of little flying insects coasted on the breeze, taking advantage of the momentum. They were coming right for her.

Wynette turned and ran. Her heels dug into the swampy ground with each step. She twisted her ankle but remained upright. Limping as fast as she could, she tried to keep ahead of the incoming swirl, but when she turned her head once more to gauge her progress, she saw it was a worthless endeavor. The critters were upon her. A cloud of little flesh-colored bugs—*are they mosquitos?* she wondered—enveloped her. Wynette waved her arms frantically, a sorry attempt to scare the things away as if they had any fear of her. There were a million of them and one of her. She was a buffet for the little blood suckers, and she could do nothing but take it.

In the distance, but not as far away as she would have liked, Wynette made out the silhouette of a large figure through the fog. It was as big as a house. Long limbs dangled off to the sides. Its top half shifted slightly as it let out another squeal. It was close enough that the sound pierced her ear drums and she lost her balance.

As she fell, she noticed another cloud of the maybe-mosquito insects emitting from the creature's maw along with its cry. By the time she splattered into the mucky ground, the little critters had covered her.

She opened her mouth to scream, but they filled the space and made their way down her throat.

The last thing to go was her vision as they attacked the whites of her eyes.

CHAPTER 10

Laughter brought Wynette back into the real world. A cackle, really. Crazed and distant, echoing through the heater vents from somewhere else in the house, yet persistent enough that she caught it in her half-conscious state.

Wynette sat up and breathed in the familiar scents of the soaps and hair products her housemates used. It was dark, but not the gray and cloudy darkness of that *other* place. Her head pounded, but she didn't feel ready to faint as she had moments earlier. Footsteps approached, but she felt no fear. The door pushed open, stopping as it hit her ankles where she'd fallen.

"Do you hear that?" Marnie asked, looking around the bathroom from the doorway before lowering her gaze. "What are your doing on the floor? Are you alright?" Before Wynette could answer, Marnie was stooped over her, reaching for her hands and helping her up to her feet.

"The strangest thing happened, but I'll tell you about it later. What is that laughter?"

Marnie tugged on her hand, pulling her into the hallway. At the other end, the rest of the girls she'd come up with crowded together at the top of the stairs. "I think it's Melinda," Kristina called out to them. "It seems this was all just some sick joke."

When Marnie and Wynette got to the other end of the hall, they headed down the stairs in a procession, meeting the other girls on the second floor and continuing down. The laughter grew louder as they arrived at the bottom landing, but there was another sound with it. Slapping. Wet. Repetitive.

"Splashing?" Hannah asked.

"Sounds like skin pounding on skin," Haley said. "Sounds like Melinda and one of her boyfriends are going at it. She's been pranking us, then."

The other girls groaned or cursed their housemate, but Wynette stayed quiet. She wasn't so sure this *was* just a prank.

They walked into the dining room, the study, the social room, but there was no sign of Melinda. The only other direction to go was the kitchen—empty—or the cellar. The basement door was still locked, just as Wynette had left it. She unbolted it, took a deep breath, and pulled the door open.

The cackling and splashing was undoubtedly coming from down there. Wynette let out her breath, took one last look at the girls cowering behind her, and descended the steps.

At the bottom, Wynette turned to face the main section of the basement. The candles had all been set back up around the circle, the flames on each one burning strong. In the very center, Melinda lay fully naked, her arms and legs outward and flailing as if she were making a snow angel. The putrid liquid that Wynette was sure was urine splashed around her. Wynette's suspicions were confirmed a moment later as more piss sprayed from between Melinda's legs and added to the puddle.

Melinda laughed wildly, continuing her repetitive movements as the girls walked over to her and stood uniformly spaced around the circle, looking down at what had once been their sister.

The eyes that stared back at them belonged to some other creature entirely.

CHAPTER 11

"We have to do something for her," Catherine cried. "How humiliating for her."

Wynette looked around the candlelit room and spotted the knitted afghan blanket draped over a pilling plaid-printed couch the girls had discarded in the basement at the end of last school year. She stepped toward it, her left foot coming down in the puddle. Her shoe slipped, but Marnie was there to catch her by the arm and keep her from taking a bath in the urine. By the time she grabbed the blanket and returned, the other girls had pulled Melinda up by her arms and were leading her out of the circle.

"Let's get you upstairs, honey," Haley said.

Wynette draped the blanket over the naked girl's shoulders and wrapped it around her front side. By the time she'd walked two steps toward the stairs, the blanket had been shrugged off by Melinda's bouncing shoulders as she laughed hysterically. Wynette picked it up and decided to let Melinda reach the top of the stairs to the kitchen before she would attempt it again.

As they entered the dining room, the lights came back on in full force. The girls winced at the sudden brightness after half an hour in the dark. In the middle of them all, Melinda collapsed. Nobody was able to keep a grip on her sweaty and urine-soaked body. She landed on the Persian rug on which the dining table sat, her head missing one of the chairs by an inch. The girls gasped in unison and stepped back as if to each show they weren't responsible for Melinda's tumble.

Melinda's eyes rolled back in her head. The whites weren't white at all, looking like the blood vessels had exploded within. She sucked in a deep breath and began to speak.

"Tuh chee seychia galla exaltia," she said, though the voice was not hers. Not exclusively, anyways, as a much grittier, deeper voice echoed it just a fraction of a second behind.

"What is she saying?" Greta whispered.

"Those are the words from the book," Haley said.

"Tsal ni alwen komoa niti," the voice spat out with much more assuredness than the way Melinda had said the words earlier in the evening. It was as if she had been fluent in the unknown language all along.

"Is she calling the spirit back or whatever?" Kristina asked. Some of the other girls whimpered at that idea.

"I don't think it ever left," Hannah said.

Catherine pointed at Wynette. "Ask Wynnie. It's her book. She's the expert at this stuff. All of this is her fault."

Wynette's breath caught in her throat along with her voice. She hadn't wanted any of this. She never asked for that book in the first place and only accepted it to keep her mother from nagging her. She hadn't wanted the book to be taken out of her closet, but her snooping roommate had insisted. She most certainly would not have willed whatever was happening with Melinda, but here they all were. There was nothing she could do about any of it now.

Protect the book.

"What?" Wynette asked.

Catherine glared at her. "I said this is all your fault. All this witchcraft and devilry. Whatever happens to Melinda, it's all on *you*."

"I heard that part." Wynette looked around the room. "Who said to protect the book?" She looked at the faces of each of the other girls, but they were all perplexed by her question.

Protect the book. This is not yet finished. Hide it well.

"Who said that?" Wynette demanded.

The voice had been a whisper. No, a collection of whispers. It hadn't even sounded female.

Am I losing my mind? she wondered. Apparently the other girls thought the same thing about her by the way they stared in horror and confusion.

Marnie walked over and pulled her in for a hug.

"It's going to be okay, Wynnie. Calm down and we'll get through this together. It's getting very late. Maybe you can get some sleep while we give Melinda a bath and take care of her."

Some of the other girls nodded in agreement while

others looked at her as if she were some lowlife trying to take the attention away from their seemingly possessed housemate.

Wynette dropped into one of the dining chairs. With Melinda's eyes returning to normal and her breathing calm, the other girls picked her up and led her up the stairs, their collective grip much stronger than before so that she could not tumble down the steps. Wynette remained in the dining room alone, listening as the group made it to the second floor and continued up to the third.

"The bathtub!" Wynette shrieked as she remembered the state it had been in. She jumped out of her chair and darted up the stairs. The girls were halfway down the third-floor hall to the bathroom. "Wait, you can't put her in there! There is blood and filth everywhere."

She squeezed past them, nearly knocking Hannah down. She pushed through the door, flipped the light switch, and turned toward the tub.

"Its..."

"It's perfectly fine," Marnie said as she came up behind her.

"But earlier when we were up here looking for Melinda... Didn't you see it when you came to get me? The blood. The hair. It..." Her voice faded off as she saw the concerned look on Marnie's face. Her own friend and roommate thought she was a lunatic.

"It's perfectly fine," Marnie repeated. Again, everyone stared at her with annoyance and disappointment, silently accusing her of trying to steal attention from Melinda's plight. "Please, Wynnie, get some rest and we'll take care of Mel. Go."

Wynette dropped her head in embarrassment and exited the overcrowded bathroom. She sulked across the hall and down one flight to where her bedroom was. The freshmen and sophomores shared the larger bedrooms on the second floor while juniors and seniors got their own bedrooms on the third. As she reached for the door of the room she shared with Marnie, she gasped and turned around. She had the unshakable feeling she was being watched, but the hallway was empty.

The book. Hide it. Protect it.

Wynette turned away from the safety of her room and took two more flights of stairs down to where the cursed book lay in a circle of chalk, candles, and urine.

CHAPTER 12

"We have to call the police," Pam said.

Greta scoffed. "Yeah, and tell them what? That we played around with witchcraft and she got possessed? They aren't going to believe it."

"They'll probably say it's alcohol poisoning or a drug overdose," Marnie said.

The young women had all taken turns throughout the night and morning watching Melinda as she slept in her bed. Perhaps *slept* wasn't the right word. From what they'd told Wynette, Melinda had tossed and turned and broke out in crazed ramblings in that unfamiliar language. Wynette hadn't been part of the rotation, as the other girls had let her sleep, perhaps as angry at her as they were terrified for Melinda. Wynette had woken up at half past seven to the sound of Marnie returning to the room to change into clean clothes. Marnie had brought her up to speed on the situation before leading her upstairs. Wynette had lain in disbelief for a minute, struggling to recall the details of the previous night. She had recalled the boredom in the social room, the feeling of betrayal from Marnie's admission she'd been snooping through Wynette's belongings where she'd found the book, and...

"The book," Wynette had whispered, sitting up in her bed.

"Yes, we looked all over for it. Nobody wanted to go down to the basement alone after last night, so Catherine, Haley, Greta, and I went together. We looked all over for your book, but it was nowhere to be found. I thought you'd taken it back to the room, but I looked everywhere. You didn't stir, even when I checked under your pillow. Hope you don't mind."

"That's so weird," Wynette had responded, and as far as she could remember at the time, she really did not have a clue what had happened to the book. It wasn't until the climb up to the third floor that she started to remember the uncanny whispers that had directed her to retrieve the book the night before. And yet, as soon as she reached the top landing, those thoughts had disappeared like the fleeting remnants of a dream upon waking.

The girls were all crowded in the hall outside of Melinda's bedroom, the door open just a crack so they could peek in at her.

"Well, if they do arrest us, at least we can all tell them Wynette is to blame," Allie said.

Kristina nodded. "I don't think it will go on our records."

"But the school will expel all of us," Hannah said. "That will *absolutely* go on our records."

"My mom is going to kill me," Haley said.

"Mine too," Pam cried. Actually wept, as if it were a sure thing that they were going to be kicked out of college for reciting a few lines of text from an old book that led to one of their sorority sisters getting possessed by some ancient mystical force.

"Gals, this is ridiculous!" Wynette shouted, startling the other girls. "This whole thing has nothing to do with the stupid book. The occult isn't real. Demons aren't real. It's all fairy tales created by religious zealots to frighten people into submission. Whatever is wrong with Melinda is something else, and we should get her to a hospital. Maybe it was a seizure. Does anyone know if she has epilepsy or some other condition?"

They all stared at her in shock. The complete silence lasted for what felt like minutes as Wynette assumed the girls had begun to see things her way, that any talk of witchcraft and possession would not just get them expelled, but also ridiculed and possibly even committed to an institution *not* of higher learning.

But then Pam spoke.

"That professor..."

Everyone shifted to stare at her questioningly.

"You know, the one from the peri... para... I don't remember what it's called. The guy that studies the ghosts. His wife teaches the class with him—she's quite gorgeous if you can get past those kind of creepy eyes, you know?"

Allie clapped her hands in excitement. "Parapsychology, yes! I remember Billy Carsten told me about them. They hunt ghosts for the Catholic Church, right? I thought Billy was just trying to scare me, but then he showed me the course catalogue in his room."

"You went into Billy Carsten's bedroom?" Hannah asked. "What a whore."

"*My* Billy Carsten?" Greta asked in a small voice.

Allie shifted uncomfortably, pretending not to hear Greta. "The Walters, that's their name. They'll totally know what to do. Let's go check the directory. I'm sure they'll be listed."

Wynette sidestepped to her left, blocking the staircase.

"Wait a minute. If we get them involved, that'll be a fast track to the administration finding out, and then we're surely in trouble. I think we should give it until this afternoon. If Melinda hasn't recovered by the time we're ready to prepare dinner, we can call them. Hell, we can call the pope if you want. Just give it a little more time."

The girls looked at each other uneasily, but Wynette was certain they each feared disciplinary action. One by one, they nodded their heads with great reluctance.

By that evening, nothing had changed. They found the Walters' phone number with no trouble, but there was no answer. They tried repeatedly through the night, but it wasn't until they gave up, slept a few hours, and tried again the next morning that John and Judith Walter returned home from a paranormal study at an abandoned hospital and answered the call from the exasperated girls.

All the while, Melinda's breathing became erratic, her voice alternated between its normal tone and something that seemed not at all of this world, and her sorority sisters' nerves shattered, their dreams for their bright futures dimming with every passing hour.

Through it all, Wynette snuck peeks behind furniture, inside drawers and cabinets and under beds, and plumbed the depths of her mind for any clue of what she had done with that book.

Perhaps she, more than the other girls, had something to fear, but she knew not what it could be.

*"O Lord Jesus Christ, I call for Your mercy to
wash over this afflicted woman. I pray for
Your blood to wash over her, to cleanse her
soul. May it seep through her pores and
deep within her insides to the very depths
of her inmost being."*

"Mighty Healer, I call for You to cast out the demon within this corrupted body. Protect her from the enemy within. Grant her Your salvation, make her white as snow and without the filth that stains her soul."

*"My Lord, Defender of Purity, Wielder of the
Shield of Faith, I beg You to drive away
the corruption in Your daughter and
defend her body from further invasion by
enemy spirts."*

"God, I call for Your mercy on this lamb, to
spare her from the rod of Satan. May You
cleanse the marrow of her bones and restore
her temple to how You intended for it
to be."

•••

No.

PART TWO

SACRA
EXORCISMI
RITUS

CHAPTER 13

The boy—a young man, really, though he'd hardly grown into his skin even at twenty-two—stalked down Blackwood Street. His eyes mostly lingered on the sidewalk in front of him, his confidence cowering in the presence of the dozens of people his own age that he passed on his way. He knew how they looked at him; after all, he was in his fourth year of college despite feeling ill-prepared to join the workforce in another year's time. He had never fit in with the frat boys and sorority girls, nor even with the dweebs and geeks that banded together and cast him out as quickly as the popular crowd. It wasn't much different from high school, really. So, he kept his head down and went about his own business, as lonely as it sometimes was. He had his books and his studies to keep him company at least.

Besides, there weren't many who would understand his passion for the dark and macabre. Hauntings and heretics. Spirits and satanic rituals. Poltergeists and possessions.

It was the last of those things that brought Arnie McCann to Blackwood Street today, an avenue he wouldn't normally stroll down with its collection of fraternity and sorority houses filling up two entire blocks. He passed house after house, the yards sprinkled with empty liquor bottles and scrunched-up beer cans from the Friday night parties he'd never been invited to and wouldn't have attended even if he had. He braved a glance at the sound of clinking glass as a team of freshmen pledges cleaned up the trash on a lawn while their upperclassmen hazed them from the shade of the porch. One of the younger boys opened his black garbage bag and puked out his hungover guts among the contents within.

There was at least some life Arnie observed at each house he passed as he trekked down the sidewalk. Each house, that is, until the brass accoutrements on the low iron gate of his destination caught his eye. *This* house was different today. Nobody was outside. No remnants of a party graced the exterior. He wiped the sweat forming on his forehead from the early autumn heat with the back of his hand, then blotted it into his sleeveless argyle sweater. He reached out to push the gate open and flinched.

It was frigid. He studied his raw fingertips. The skin had nearly ripped off. The boy held his hand over the black iron bars of the gate and soaked in the iciness. He stepped back and looked around. The morning sun was out, the sky blue with only the sparsest of wispy clouds.

He moved in, using his shoe to push the gate open. It creaked as it swung inward and he stepped through. He moved aside to let it swing closed again and took a moment for his eyes to adjust.

The yard was dim. A low fog blocked out the sky.

"Impossible," Arnie whispered. He glanced around at his surroundings. The blades of grass were covered in frost. The trees were bare and surrounded with rotting piles of leaves. The house loomed over him, a Craftsman structure with tacked-on additions sticking out like warts. Every window was fogged. The lower portions of roof he could see were frozen over.

"Impossible," he repeated, and yet it was far from the strangest thing he'd witnessed in his relatively short life.

The boy took the steps to the porch slowly, careful not to slip. The porch floorboards groaned under his feet as if ready to give up the ghost and collapse under him. He stopped in front of the door and cocked his head, listening for any signs of life. No laughter. No singing. No seniors barking orders to their plebeian underclassmen.

He took a deep breath and reached for the knob. Warning signs flashed in his mind.

Turn back.

Leave while you can.

Run.

Arnie ignored the premonitions, opened the front door, and stepped in to his fate.

CHAPTER 14

He anticipated a frigid breeze to accompany the swinging door, as if he were stepping into an industrial freezer. The shock of a heat-wave greeted him instead.

Arnie had never been inside a sorority house. Half-expecting pajama parties and open bottles of wine on every surface, what he instead saw as he stepped from the foyer into the front room was a fairly clean home that would have made his grandmother proud. On one wall, book bags were neatly set into a row of cubbies under a shelf of textbooks. Three writing desks sat against the opposite wall, one with a typewriter, the others with orderly stacked piles of paper and a cup of pens and pencils on each. In the fetishization of sorori-ties and fraternities, he admitted to himself, he hadn't considered that their members were students just like him, working hard between social gatherings to main-tain their studies and prepare for their eventual careers in the real world.

He breathed in deep, a confidence entering him like a spirit. He stopped in the middle of the room on a red Persian rug with a paisley pattern and cocked his head. Listening.

No lively conversation, nor laughter. Still, there was not complete silence. At first, he mistook the sound for buzzing, or the white noise of a television with a broken antenna. He continued his way through the room, under a curved archway, and into a dining room.

To his left, through another arch, was a living room with three sofas and an assortment of mismatched accent chairs pushed together in roughly a circle. Nine students sat with heads bowed, whispering nearly in unison as they stared down at papers in their laps. Standing in the center, an antique leather-bound book in her hands, was a woman a few years their senior.

Judith Walter turned to face the newcomer, not hesitating in her quiet recitation of the words on the page. The young man knew her just well enough to decipher the concern on her face. He locked eyes with her for a moment, and then she turned away, raising her voice slightly louder than before. A floorboard creaked when he stepped into the room, causing a few of the sorority sisters to look up and stutter in their words. Judith shifted her open book into one hand and waved at the girls to continue reading.

Arnie studied the faces of those whose backs were not turned to him. Every one of them had red eyes and cheeks raw from wiping away tears. Crumpled tissues or soiled handkerchiefs sat on laps or between couch cushions. A tragedy had befallen them.

He remained standing there, attempting to make out the words. They alternated between passages in English and Latin. Scriptures from the Bible mixed with prayers. The words sounded as if they were unfamiliar to most of them, but they stumbled through the Latin well enough with Judith leading them. Time passed, perhaps a minute or perhaps five, before he realized he had fallen into a daze, a rhythmic cloud of whispers hypnotizing him into a waking slumber.

And then the voice called out.

"Judith, where is that good-for-nothing porky kid? I need some damn help right now!"

Judith looked up at the young man, embarrassment on her face. Without breaking from the words she recited, Judith cocked her head up toward the ceiling, pointing him away with her chin. He nodded and began to step away from the group prayer session when he noticed one of the girls had shifted her head to look at him. Arnie thought he recognized her. That fiery orange hair would stand out anywhere. Her green eyes burned into him until he pulled himself away from the archway and out of sight. Past the dining room, he found the staircase that led up to the bedrooms where the sorority girls slept.

Under any other circumstances, Arnie was certain he'd never visit such a place, but this was not an ordinary day.

SOMETHING STIRRED INSIDE WYNETTE'S HEAD LIKE A scorpion fish, stinging at her brain, causing spikes of fear within. The way the boy had looked at her...

Had he seen something in her face?

Could her guilt be read so easily?

From another part of the circle of women, Judith Walter cleared her throat. The other girls stuttered in their recitation of the prayers.

"Keep going, ladies," Judith ordered. "We have the power here, not Satan." Her eyes met Wynette's, causing sweat to pour down Wynette's forehead. The older woman's eyes told a story of their own, one of surviving similar events.

Of coming out *changed*.

Scarred by what she had experienced during previous exorcisms.

This would be no easy feat for any of them, even Wynette and her sisters who had no other role than to recite these prayers.

And yet, Wynette felt she had one other course of action.

I can run away from here. Far away. Never come back. Never see these girls again.

But that thing swimming in her head insisted that she stay and witness the power that it held.

THE SMELL HIT ARNIE AS HE REACHED THE SECOND-floor landing.

"Up here, you dolt!" came an angry voice from one

floor higher. The young man sighed and continued his ascent. The stench grew more rancid as he climbed, just as the heat became more unbearable the higher he went.

The third floor had a lower ceiling than the first two levels. A corridor ran down either side of the landing, with three closed doors on each wall along the length and a doorway into a bathroom to cap off the far end. The door nearest him was open just a crack, the odd light seeping through interrupted by a shadow.

"Come on in," John Walter beckoned as he pulled the door open. His wide-shouldered form blocked the young man's view of the interior of the room, perhaps by design to keep him from running off at the sight of the horrors within. "Welcome to your very first exorcism, Arnold."

CHAPTER 15

Arnie stepped into a sorority girl's bedroom for the first time, inhaling an uncharacteristic whiff of body odor from John Walter, a man usually so suave and composed. The man's usual pompadour-styled hair stood at all angles in disarray. Sweat soaked through his thin white T-shirt, darkening not just under his arms but down his chest and spine. John's suspenders hung loosely on either side of his slacks, which were rolled halfway up his calves, while his button-up shirt had been discarded under a desk.

"Did Judith catch you up on everything?" John asked. His voice had a rasp to it, worn to exhaustion from whatever he'd been doing up here.

"No," Arnie said softly. "She was..." He trailed off at the sight on the bed.

"It would have been easier if she had," John said. He grabbed Arnie's shoulder and directed him to a mahogany chair. "Sit down and let me bring you up to speed."

Arnie complied, though every synapse in his body fired off and screamed, *"run!"* His eyes remained glued to the girl tied to the bedposts like the cover of a raunchy romance paperback from the drug store.

"Eyes on me, Casanova," John taunted as he snapped his fingers in front of Arnie's face. The girl had been still since he walked in, but just as his eyes peeled away from her, she shifted on the bed. The thin sheet over her lower half slipped off, revealing legs bruised purple and a loose skirt bunched up at her waist with nothing below. He gasped and turned to John.

"Sorry," he whispered.

"Your fear is understandable, Arnie, but this ain't the time for it. The enemy feeds off negative emotions, and its favorite flavor in a time like this is fear from those feigning toughness. Look at me, boy. Do I look afraid?"

Arnie studied him and saw right through his strongman act, but he didn't want to say so. "No," he lied with little conviction.

"That's right. This ain't my first rodeo. Judith and I have had two dozen experiences more difficult than this one is going to be. Still, you're going to look at the form of that girl on the bed and think there's no way she's dangerous, but you'll be wrong. Don't turn your back on her. Understand me so far?"

Arnie nodded, not wanting to point out that John's back was turned to her at that very moment.

"Good. Now, Judith has a prayer circle going with the other girls to set up a holy veil in this house and cast out any spirits not already embedded in this poor gal. I can already feel it working. You noticed the heat, no doubt."

"Yes," Arnie said. "It was the complete opposite in the front yard, though."

John pointed to a puddle on the worn hardwood floor. "It was just as frosty inside when we got here until they started praying with Judith. In the demon's anger and fear, the heat came over us like an oven. Melted the ice right off the windows. *That* is how you know we're going to win this one."

A whimper sounded out from the form on the bed. John turned and Arnie followed his gaze. Sweat-matted hair split just enough to reveal sad eyes. Her face scrunched in a pleading look aimed directly at Arnie. His heart skipped a beat.

"Please," she sobbed in a tiny, high-pitched voice. "Save me from this lunatic. He's hurting me. You have to do something."

John turned back to Arnie and rolled his eyes. "Ignore her."

Arnie tried to ignore her, but the sorrowful cries continued.

"So what happened here," John explained, "is quite a common case. One of the well-meaning parents of a sorority gal gifted her daughter an occult book on conjuring spirits. Allegedly an archaic volume she found at an estate sale. She thought it would be good fun, a way to get her daughter to engage with the sorority sisters she'd been having a hard time fitting in with.

"The girls all swear they didn't believe in any of it, that it was all just for fun. That's not how it works, though. Willing souls and open minds are needed for demonic spirits to enter them. They were all just too afraid to admit to each other, worried that they'd be mocked for believing in the supernatural.

"On Friday night, instead of gallivanting around the parties held by their neighbors, these girls drew the curtains, lit some candles, and sat in a circle on the cellar floor. They followed some of the conjuring rituals described in the book. Chanted words in an ancient language."

A creak in the hallway drew Arnie's attention to the door as Judith pushed her way in. She stood silently for a moment, observing the girl in bondage, before continuing John's tale. The couple switched off, describing the bits and pieces of the story as the sorority sisters had told it to them. When they got to the attempted phone calls on the previous night, Arnie interrupted.

"So where is the book? Does it have some kind of reverse incantation we can recite?"

John's jaw dropped as he looked at Arnie with what the boy felt was ridicule. Arnie gulped with embarrassment.

"*Reverse... incantation?*" John asked in an incredulous tone, drawing out each word to accentuate their stupidity.

"John, be kind. He's new to all this," his wife said as she crossed the room to stand over the girl on the bed.

John's expression softened. He nodded his head. "Right. Well, Arnold, I'm afraid it's just not as simple as that. The book is nowhere to be found. The girls claim they searched the entire house yesterday but it never turned up."

"Is that... Is it normal for a book like this to disappear after a..." Arnie wasn't sure the right word for it, but tried anyway, hoping he wouldn't be mocked for it. "After a *possession?*"

"No. It is possible that Melinda here was able to hide it somewhere they haven't thought to look. After all, she moved all around the house that night undetected while the other girls turned the place upside down looking for her, only to eventually show up in the place they had started it all. There's no telling what she is—"

Girlish giggling cut off John's words. He and Arnie glanced over at her. Even though Judith stood at her side, the girl looked past her. Those eyes, dilated and eerily yellow on the edges, bore straight into Arnie. The laughter from the possessed girl grew into a mad cackle, which morphed into a coughing fit. Bloody tears dripped from her eyes and down her temples onto the pillow.

"All we do know is that she's been like this ever since," Judith concluded. "Compromised. Possessed, as you said."

"And now we're going to save her," John said, turning back to Arnie with a smile. "I hope you're ready, boy."

CHAPTER 16

John popped the latches open on a black briefcase atop a dresser in the bedroom. Arnie had seen the case before. It was the same one John had plopped down onto the desk at the front of the cavernous lecture hall each Monday and Wednesday evening over the last few weeks, and each Tuesday and Thursday evening the previous semester. In both classes, the hall had been packed the first two or three sessions, with students eager to witness the infamous figure leading the lectures.

The ghost hunter.

The exorcist.

The *freak*.

All but a few would drop the courses at that point, satisfied by what they'd seen, bored by what they'd heard. Arnie, though, had continued with the classes, taking them as seriously as the upper-level courses of his actual major, history. As John had pointed out in the previous semester's Introduction to Parapsychology course, Arnie was the top student by far. Not that it was a surprise to Arnie, who spent every moment outside of classes furthering his studies and striving to be top of the class, no matter the subject. Academic achievements had always come naturally to the young man. It was just a bonus, then, that John Walter's classes so acutely matched Arnie's actual interests. The subjects began to explain some of the things Arnie had witnessed during his youth in his hometown of Raventree Hollow.

The latches unclasped, John pivoted his torso to face Melinda on the bed, with Judith standing over her. The married couple locked eyes and nodded in unison, then both stared down at the girl. Arnie watched in confusion.

"Prepare yourself," John said softly to Arnie at his side. He slowly lifted the lid of the case, his eyes fixed on Melinda. The girl remained there, her eyes fixed on Arnie. Everyone stood still for a few moments. Silent.

Judith turned back to her husband, a look of confusion on her face. "Didn't you bring everything?"

"Of course I did, darling." John grabbed the case and tilted it so everyone could see its contents: two worn leather-bound books, a glass vial of liquid, and a wooden crucifix with a brass statuette of Jesus affixed to it. The couple looked back at the girl, who remained staring at Arnie.

Arnie felt his companions' stares on him as well. "What?" he asked.

"I've never seen anything like it," Judith said. "It's

like she's so fixated on him that she's protected from the power of the cross."

"Pfft," John scoffed. He clanked the case back onto the dresser and pulled out the crucifix. Wielding it in front of him like a shield, he rushed across the room toward the young woman on the bed. "Look right here and study it closely. The power of Christ in my hand. Flee from this place right now, demon, before this gets any harder for you."

The girl broke her stare at Arnie and looked up at the older man. Her face scrunched, her eyes narrowed, and she began to weep.

"It's working," Judith observed. "She..."

Her voice faded, overpowered by Melinda's cries morphing into mocking laughter.

"You... You think..." Melinda's laughter broke up her attempts at speaking a whole sentence, but Arnie noticed in just those words that the girl's voice was both soft and sweet yet low and dark. Two voices at once. "You think that little toy is going to hurt me?" Her laughter turned into a roar.

The scowl grew on John's face. He thrust the crucifix inches in front of Melinda's face.

"Look at it!" Spittle flew from John's lips and rained down on her. "Christ will conquer you and send you back to the depths of Hell. Now release this girl from your grip!"

Melinda snarled and sat up as much as she was able, making to bite at the crucifix or at John. Her teeth grazed his fingertips that wrapped around the cross. He yanked his hand away but dropped the cross. It plummeted to the mattress, bounced, and thudded to the hardwood floor.

"God damn it," John shouted. He brought his fingers to his mouth and sucked at the wound like a small child.

"Careful, holy man," Melinda mocked. "You shouldn't take your lord's name in vain."

John stepped away from the bed and toward the dresser. "Pick that up, would you Judith?"

His wife complied, going down to her knees at the bedside and reaching for the crucifix. She grunted as her fingers failed to grasp it. "Something's not right."

John arrived at the dresser where his case sat. He turned his head to Arnie and looked at the young man with disdain. "Are you just planning to stand there all day like some helpless idiot? Go give my wife a hand."

"I... Okay." Arnie jogged to Judith's side and knelt down. His fingers found no purchase on the religious item. It was stuck to the floor as if it had been glued to the spot. "How is that possible?" he muttered. Arnie tried digging his fingernails under the edges to no avail.

The girl giggled again. "You can just ask me politely to release it," she said in that uncanny dual voice.

"Um, would... Will you release the cross?" he asked. "Please?"

It spun in a circle, then flew upward, narrowly missing Arnie's face. The crucifix sliced into the ceiling, little bits of drywall flaking down. It hung perfectly upside-down just over the bed.

"Oops," Melinda said.

"Enough playing around." John turned away from his

case and marched toward them with the vial in his hand. "It's time for the holy water."

The girl squirmed at this. "No," she begged. "Please, anything but that. Anything. Please!"

Her scream filled the room, both the highest pitch and lowest rumble Arnie could ever remember hearing.

AFTER JUDITH HAD LEFT THE SOCIAL ROOM TO JOIN her husband and that boy upstairs, the voice of each girl in the circle had faded into eventual silence.

Wynette looked around at her housemates, absorbing their fears and anxieties. Her own guilt was there, but something overshadowed it. Something that came from a dark place within her, rising up from the muck of her innards. It came from the same place as the smile one must suppress at another's grief, the eye roll at someone's displeasure, the jealousy felt over a friend's success, the greed innate in all.

She felt pride. Excitement. Accomplishment.

Just as quickly as those feelings had risen in her, they faded away at the sound of the screams from above.

No, she told herself, *that's not who I am. It can't be.*

And yet, she knew it was.

CHAPTER 17

Melinda cut off the scream as John arrived at her side and flicked what he had called holy water at her face. Drops sprinkled onto her cheeks and forehead. Instead of dripping down the sides of her head, they sizzled like oil on a burning skillet and dissipated. Raw pink welts took their place.

"Is that going to leave scars?" Arnie asked.

"Her entire soul will be scarred. Her lovely skin should be the least of your worries." John continued to pelt her with the contents of the vial. Her breathing rate increased, her chest rising up and down with intensity. She let out a moan of ecstasy, undeniably sexual. Arnie stumbled backward a step. He felt his cheeks heating and turning red with embarrassment and unwelcome titillation.

"I don't think it's working," Judith said to her husband. "This isn't right."

"Oh it is *so* right," Melinda said, her voice doubled

with that uncannily low and evil tone. "Keep going, holy man. Make me scream."

"Wicked beast, leave this body immediately," John ordered. He capped the vial and returned it to the case before sitting down on a padded stool at the vanity next to the dresser.

"Giving up so soon, holy man?" Melinda asked.

"I'm no clergyman, wench. Quit it with that *holy man* talk already."

Arnie looked at him in surprise. "You mean you aren't sanctioned to perform exorcisms? I thought you had to be."

Judith crossed the room and stood next to her husband. She wrapped her fingers around his shoulders and began massaging him. She spoke for John.

"We have had dozens of cases in the last several years where exorcisms were necessary to cast demonic entities out of victims. In all but one case, we had a local priest or Protestant minister with us to perform the act. While the effectiveness is improved when performed by a man of the cloth, my husband is quite capable and well-versed. The first time he had to perform one himself, he had no trouble."

"There are plenty of churches around here," Arnie said. "Do you need me to go to one for help?"

John shook his head furiously. "It's not that easy, kid. They need permission from higher up in the chain. Archdiocese, even the Vatican depending on the situation. We don't have time for that. This girl is young. Vulnerable. The demon within her will destroy her soul and break her body before the bureaucracy can even get around to picking up the phone." He reached for one of the books in his case and held it up. "All we need is the Word of God, a little bravery, and a whole lot of faith. We have it all right here."

Arnie studied the man's face. Even though he didn't know John Walter outside of school prior to this fateful morning, he'd seen John's various moods and expressions over a semester and a half, dealing with unruly college students, disengaged pupils, and nonbelievers. He had gotten to know John's demeanors and exaggerated outbursts of anger.

Right now what he saw was a man full of doubt and low on confidence.

This was not going to be easy at all.

CHAPTER 18

"But God shall wound the head of his enemies," John read out of his well-worn Bible, standing at the foot of the bed on which Melinda lay in bondage, "and the hairy scalp of such an one as goeth on still in his trespasses. The Lord said, I will bring again from Bashan, I will bring my people again from the depths of the sea: that thy foot may be dipped in the blood of thine enemies, and the tongue of the dogs in the same."

He balanced the Bible in his left hand and reached out with his right. Arnie uncapped the vial of holy water and handed it to him. John sprinkled some on Melinda's uncannily purple feet, which caused her to flinch. He then moved around the bed and sprinkled it on her forehead. Unlike the first time, there was no burning of skin. It didn't hit her like a corrosive acid this time, but as mere drops of water.

"Be gone from this young woman, demon. Leave her

at once in the name of Jesus." John took a step back and repeated the commands. Everyone stood in silence, watching the poor girl on the bed. Her tears were no longer bloody, and they mixed in with the drops of holy water.

Melinda lifted her head and looked into Arnie's eyes.

"Please, Arnie," she begged through sobs, "make him stop this. Untie me."

"I can't," Arnie said. "I'm sorry." He studied his companions, hoping they'd speak up on his behalf, but they just watched the girl lie there, the demon having hidden somewhere within her.

"Don't you want me?" she asked. Melinda shifted her knees as much as she was able to, knocking the light sheet off of her and sending it slipping off the bed. Her bare thighs rubbed together, then moved them apart.

Arnie gasped and looked away.

"I'm yours if you want me," she continued, the unnaturally deep voice missing. "You just have to save me from these wicked charlatans."

"Ignore her," Judith commanded. She leaned forward and pulled the sheet back over Melinda's lower half.

"Am I that bad, Arnie? Tell a girl she's pretty, won't you?"

Arnie looked at her face. Her lips were pursed in a pouty way that would have been cute at any other time. She batted her eyelashes.

"Tell me, Arnie," she said again, this time with a little edge.

"You... You..."

The upper half of her body shot up as much as it was able with her restraints. "Tell me I am pretty, Arnie boy," she growled, the demon's low voice returning and echoing under her own.

Arnie took a step backward, tripping on a book that had been tossed aside. He fell to the floor, landing ungracefully on his backside. The sheet flew off of Melinda, hovering above her body while she arched herself upward. Urine gushed from the possessed girl like a fountain. He rolled away, narrowly avoiding it.

The demon's laughter came out of the young lady's mouth, too cruel and deep to be her own. John crossed the room and exchanged his Bible for the other book. He thumbed through it to a dogeared page and recited its contents in what Arnie assumed was Latin. The demon's laughter mocked him, rising in volume. John shouted his words to match, repeating a line over and over. His voice grew hoarse and he threw the book back into his briefcase in frustration.

"Calm down, John. You'll give it more power," Judith warned. She wrapped her arms around her husband, giving him no choice but to hug her back. They remained that way for half of a minute while the demon's laughter faded in apparent exhaustion.

Arnie got back to his feet and shuffled awkwardly in the silence. "So, um, was that Latin?"

Judith's hair blew outward as John spoke through it. "Ancient languages sound more powerful, don't they?" It was a silly question that Arnie wanted to giggle at, but the demon beat him.

"Ha! You think that Latin is ancient?" it mocked. "I

know languages that predate this pathetic world of yours."

"Impossible, beast," John said, breaking his wife's embrace. "Our Lord created this world before you were ever conceived. There were no languages before that."

"This world and your so-called god are just a blink of an eye to me. Your kind are so ignorant, holy man," the demon goaded. "Merely *speaking* the words I know would bring catastrophic destruction to this entire city. Your little brains would burst within your heads and bleed out of your ears and nostrils. Your eyes would melt like candle wax to the floor. Of course, that would destroy my host, so I'll keep the words to myself. For now, anyway."

"I am sick and tired of your blasphemous mouth," John shouted. He grabbed a track-and-field trophy off of the bedside table. Its base was a solid rectangle of marble. He lifted it up, ready to bring it down on Melinda's face. The piercing scream that came out of the girl's mouth sounded like her own.

"Stop!" Arnie yelled as he pounced forward and grabbed John's arm. "You can't hurt the girl. She doesn't deserve this."

John pushed back. "She helped bring this thing into the world. These kids are so damn irresponsible. Maybe some extra scars will remind her the next time she even *thinks* about dabbling in the occult again. Satan is not a force to—"

"Satan?" the entity in Melinda called before breaking into another bout of laughter. "I am no force of your little Satan, you fool. This would be so much easier for you if that were so, wouldn't it? Looks like you'll have to put a little extra work in today, holy man."

"John?" Judith asked. Arnie pulled the trophy from John's hand and stepped away, but both men's eyes were glued to Judith. The concern on her face echoed onto their own. "What if it's telling the truth? What if it isn't a satanic entity?"

"What are you talking about? What else could it possibly be?"

"You poor fool," it mocked.

Judith turned and walked toward the door. "Come on, let's get some fresh air and check on the other girls. We can all use a break."

As hot as the rest of the house was, Arnie still felt a relative breeze as she opened the door for them. The smell lessened as they trekked into the hallway and down the stairs.

On the first floor, they walked into the room of crying girls. Their prayer circle had stopped, emotions apparently overtaking the sisters. Judith waved the men away as she went over to console them.

"Come on," John said, pulling at Arnie's sweater vest. He led the younger man to the kitchen and opened the refrigerator. "Bingo." He retrieved two cans of light beer, tossed one to Arnie, and walked out the back door.

The pair sat on the steps of the rear porch, the unnatural coolness a relief. Arnie's sweat-soaked armpits went cold within minutes as they sipped wordlessly at their beverages.

"So I've been thinking," John said, breaking the

silence. "Maybe this demon realizes he has the upper hand on us."

"You still think it's a demon?" Arnie asked.

John turned and glared at him. "This is exactly what I'm getting at. What did you say your religion was? Back home in Backwater Ravine or whatever you said your little incest-filled town was called?"

"I don't think we discussed religion at all," Arnie replied. He set the beer down and belched. He'd only had alcoholic beverages a couple times before, but never found them enjoyable in taste or function. This time, however, it seemed to do the job, cooling him and refreshing him after what felt like a marathon of an hour in the scorching room upstairs.

"Tell me the place you come from at least has a little chapel or something," John said.

"Raventree Community Church, but my family wasn't really religious. My grandmother went to their events for the social aspects, but not to the regular services. She's the one who raised me, and she said organized religion is for the feeble minded. She said they are sheep, and that we have to be wolves."

"Interesting. So are you?"

"Huh?"

"Are you a wolf, Arnold?" John lifted his head and howled. It was so ridiculous that Arnie couldn't help but laugh.

"I'm just... I mean, I believe in things that science hasn't yet explained. I haven't *discounted* religion entirely, if that's what you're getting at."

"Right, so not a Catholic, not even a *Protestant*,"

John said, emphasizing his disgust at that last word. He sighed and shook his head. "You see, demons feed off this kind of thing. They get their power from disharmony."

"I thought you said they get power from those who believe? So shouldn't it be the opposite from those who don't?"

"See, there's truth in that as well, but disharmony is a different kind of weapon it uses. Discord, the weapon of Satan. It's like a man and woman marrying when they're unequally yoked. It's just not going to work out. You ever know a couple like that? How'd it work out for them?"

He had, in fact, known one in particular. The pastor of the church in his town had been in a relationship of some sort with a pagan woman most folks referred to as the town witch. And the pastor had died in a brutal fashion. That was neither here nor there, however, so Arnie shook his head.

"Well, we're seeing it right now. You're the weak link, I'm afraid, but the unfortunate thing for us both is that I need you here. I can't do this with just Judith. She's too vulnerable when she's the target of a demon, and this demon has fortunately found itself attracted to you. So, we're going to roll with that."

"Like, you're going to use me as bait?" Arnie asked.

John smiled and knocked his beer into Arnie's, meaning it as an uninvited *cheers*, but instead it pushed the can out of Arnie's trembling hands, spilling the remaining contents onto the younger man's slacks.

"Now you're catching on, kid."

"Great," Arnie muttered as John stood up and walked back inside to the kitchen. He sighed. "Just great."

CHAPTER 19

Judith met John and Arnie in the kitchen on their way back from their breather out on the porch. Through the doorway behind her, Arnie could see a few of the sorority sisters congregating in the dining room, tears lining their cheeks like snail tracks. The one with red hair met his eyes. He saw something *off* in her gaze and his breath cut short in his lungs. He looked away quickly.

"I'm going to take the ladies out for a soda down at the drug store," Judith told her husband.

"Are you sure that's such a good idea?" John asked. "Their demeanor will bring down the place. People will ask questions. We don't want to bring any attention to this situation."

"They need to get out of this house before they snap. It'll do them some good," Judith insisted.

"The entity won't be able to feed off their fear and sorrow the farther away they get from here," Arnie chimed in. The couple turned to look at him, Judith with an inquisitive look and John with a scowl.

John opened his mouth, ready to scold the boy for speaking out of turn, but Judith put a hand on his chest and spoke first.

"That's quite intuitive, Arnold," she said. She turned to her husband with eyebrows raised. "And you know he's right. The demon laps it up like a milkshake. He's energized by it. Speaking of milkshakes, can I bring one back for either of you?"

An ice-cold milkshake sounded heavenly to Arnie in that moment, what with the scorching interior of the house, and he nearly said so when John scoffed. "Arnold and I found the beer these ladies have been stashing away. Good enough for us."

Judith frowned at him and pointed a finger playfully. "You, sir, need to be in your best frame of mind. No more beer for you. Arnold, make sure my husband has only water or coffee from here on out."

With that, she turned and led the flock of young ladies to the front yard and out into the world they'd been hidden away from since what had befallen their dear friend Melinda.

"Oh, Arnie dear," a singsong voice floated down from the stairwell as soon as the front door closed. "Don't keep a girl waiting or she might lose her interest."

He flashed a look of horror at John, but the man only smirked. "Go on, lover boy. I'll be right behind you after I get the coffee brewing."

Arnie sighed and turned away. He regretted every

step up the two flights of stairs. As the stench grew, so did the dread he felt deep within his gut. This wasn't the first time he had faced something supernatural, though John and Judith did not know that. His hometown of Raventree Hollow was a hotspot for paranormal activity, something the locals kept secret so as not to draw the attention of predatory hucksters and frauds. Of people like John and Judith Walter.

No, he told himself as he stepped onto the top floor landing, *they mean well. They're as earnest as possible in all this. At least, they* believe *they're helping people like Melinda.*

A creaking sound broke his thoughts. Ahead of him, the door to Melinda's room was open just a crack. He took a deep breath, trying his hardest not to gag from the stench, and pushed it all the way open.

He gasped.

The bed was empty.

He peeked behind the door, under the desk, next to the dresser. All empty. The closet was open and revealed no place to hide.

"In here, big stud," her voice came from down the hall. It held none of the demon's gruff timbre, nor was it as innocent as the pleading tone she'd used on him earlier. He stepped back into the hall. The other bedroom doors were still closed. The bathroom at the other end of the long hall was illuminated. "Don't keep a girl waiting," she called.

Arnie looked down the stairwell. John wasn't on his way up yet, and he could faintly hear the sound of items being moved around in the fridge. Hunting for more beer, most likely. Arnie sighed and made his way down the hall to the bathroom. As he approached, the quality of the air changed completely. The humidity was stronger, thicker. The stench was still there but masked under what reminded him of the hodgepodge of flowers from the nursery he walked past daily in his younger years back in his hometown. There was a light splashing sound. He stepped inside.

Melinda lay in the tub immediately to his right. She was fully naked, submerged in water filled nearly to the brim.

How did we not hear the water running from downstairs? he wondered. He struggled to keep his eyes off her, but they were pulled toward her like a pair of strong magnets. The filth had been washed off her. She looked perfect, like any other naked girl Arnie had fantasized about in his dreams. He'd never actually seen a woman fully nude before, unless one counted the pictures in biology textbooks and medical volumes he had snuck peeks at during his youth as a volunteer in the Raventree Hollow Public Library.

She lifted a hand from the water and curled a finger, beckoning for him to come closer. "Your gateway to a thousand worlds," she said in a seductive tone.

He took a step toward her involuntarily before stopping himself as the words registered.

That phrase... How could she know it?

It was something the librarians back home had said to greet patrons, a tradition he partook in both as a visitor and a volunteer at the library.

"You know, Arnie, I've watched you for a long time," she said. "I sat in the back row of your calculus class last semester. Saw how your mind worked like a human encyclopedia, reciting mathematical theories as if they were engraved on your brain. It drove me wild, even if I never worked up the courage to talk to you. Thank goodness for second chances. Why don't you take off those sexy spectacles and slip out of those clothes? Come on and join me in here."

"I..." He took one more step, the tip of his shoe bumping the clawed foot of the tub. The sane part of his mind fired off warnings, told him to turn and run, call to John for help. The carnal part of his mind didn't, and he couldn't push it away. Something moved him beyond his free will. His hands went to his belt, unbuckling it with shaky fingers. He pulled at it, bringing it out of the loops of his slacks.

A hand grabbed his wrist, snapping him from the demon's power.

"Just what we needed," John said as he yanked the belt away from Arnie. He pushed the younger man aside and reached for Melinda's arms. She screamed in frustration as John wrapped the belt around her wrists, locking her hands together. "Help me get her out of this tub, kid."

"I... Yes, sir."

Arnie reached down, realizing for the first time how the water was greenish yellow and murky. It looked like a swamp, nothing like what he saw as he gazed upon the young woman's naked body. He saw the welts on her ankles and around the wrists on either side of the belt. Her legs were bruised. Cuts lined her arms. Dried blood caked on her chin and breasts, and burned pocks from the reaction to the holy water dotted her entire face. Her hair was greasy and knotted. The stench returned in full force and Arnie turned to the toilet and vomited, narrowly pulling the lid up in time.

The entity had tricked him, and Arnie had let it into his head.

CHAPTER 20

Wynette followed eight of her sorority sisters through the door held open by Judith Walter. Patrons of Carmichael's Corner turned at the approach of the somber bunch marching toward the soda counter like a funeral procession. Gregory Calvertson, a fellow sophomore Wynette had gotten to know quite well in her general education courses and at Alpha Kappa Pi frat parties, was shoveling a scoop of mint chocolate chip ice cream into a waffle cone for a patron.

"I'll be with you ladies in just a moment," he said as he finished helping a pair of middle school boys achieve their sugar rush. A few of the girls walked over to the glass case overlooking the ice cream flavors while others plopped down in the largest booth. Wynette gazed around the store at the patrons.

Look at all of them, going about their business like there wasn't a portal to Hell cracked open just two blocks from here, she thought as she eyed an elderly woman trying on blush at the makeup counter and a half-dozen folks standing in line to pick up their prescription drugs. *The devil may be among them right now, and they don't know any better.*

"Well, what will it be, Wynette?" Gregory asked. His smile was the closest thing to joy she'd seen in the last two days, and she nearly melted at the sight of it. Despite everything, she returned it with a smile of her own.

"Happy Sunday, Greg," she said in a voice more normal and cheerful than she expected. She turned to take in the dour sight of her housemates and scrambled for an excuse. "We've been studying hard for midterms all weekend, so I thought the girls could use something to liven up what's left of today."

"I'm treating," Judith said from behind her.

Gregory's stunned expression didn't surprise Wynette. "Mrs. Walter offered to tutor us, and we took her up on the offer. We're very grateful."

"Gee, I didn't know you gals were taking those parapsychology classes." Gregory looked accusingly at Wynette as if she were tainted.

"Oh, no," Judith interjected. She had apparently grown used to the disapproval of most people over the years. "I'm proficient in many more subjects than that. I have a degree in European history, you know."

Gregory put on a fake smile and nodded. "Got it. So, what can I get you gals?" Wynette waved her sitting sisters over and everyone placed their orders. A few minutes later, they crammed into the booth and pulled up a few extra chairs to accommodate everyone. They'd been sitting in a circle all day at the house, and now were doing the same in the drug store, though instead of whispered prayers, the only sounds coming from the young ladies were slurps through straws and the occasional sighs. Judith broke the pattern by clearing her throat.

"I'm so proud of you all," the older woman among them said. "What you are facing is not something many throughout this world—throughout history, really—will ever have to experience. I've seen people broken by less than what is afflicting Melinda, support systems crumbling from fear and sorrow. Not you girls, though. You are brave and persistent and exactly what Melinda needs to get through this situation."

No reaction came from the girls, just the sounds of straws sucking up sugar-filled dairy. Wynette couldn't take any more of her milkshake. She set her tall glass on the sticky Formica table, wiped the condensation off on her skirt, and eyed the other girls. Her gaze stopped on Pam, the fear most easily readable on this freshman of all the girls. Pam slurped loudly through the straw, but her eyes were locked on Wynette. Pam stopped sucking in the milkshake mid-inhale. Her cheeks ballooned. Her upper body rocked, and she began to choke.

"Oh my gosh!" Catherine cried as her roommate heaved. "Pammie, are you okay?" The other girls vacated the booth to give Pam space, anticipating the coagulated milk and sugar and chocolate and saliva that came spraying out of her mouth. Judith reached over the table and pulled a wad of napkins from the silver dispenser and held them in front of Pam's mouth.

"I'll take her to the bathroom," Wynette offered. She put one knee on the bench and leaned in toward Pam, her right arm extending over the girl's shoulders. Pam flinched at the touch, but Wynette persisted, guiding her out of the booth and toward the bathroom while the other girls made sounds of shock behind them.

"Let go of me," Pam said once they pushed through the door of the restroom. Her glare was as accusatory as it was angry.

"What's wrong? It wasn't me who made you choke."

"No, Wynnie, but it was you who brought that stupid book into our house. You *corrupted* us with that!"

Wynette noticed then that Pam had brought the milkshake with her into the bathroom and had brought the straw back to her lips.

"I think you should take a break from the shake, Pam," she attempted, but the freshman ignored her and took a long pull from the straw. Her shoulders bucked again. She pulled the glass away from her face, a string of saliva stretching from her lips to the striped straw.

No, not saliva.

It was blood red.

It wriggled and writhed.

Pam's choking resumed. The glass slipped from her hands and shattered on the checkered tile floor into a pool of chocolate ice cream, milk, and jagged shards.

The crimson strand dangled, twisted, moved its way up between Pam's lips. She reached for it and pulled.

And pulled.

It stretched like something gummy, but it had

purchase somewhere in the girl's throat. Whimpers emitted from the girl, then gurgling, then wheezing, stilted breaths. Pam's skin flushed with a blue tint. She could no longer breathe.

Wynette stepped forward, ignoring the crunching of glass under her shoe. She grabbed the strand between Pam's clutched fists and helped to yank it out of the girl's throat. After three attempts, it broke free, flew out, and slapped against Wynette's face with a wet *thwack*.

Pamela stumbled back against the sink, turned, and vomited. Wynette held the strand out in front of her face to get a better look.

It wasn't crimson at all. It was orange. It was a braid of hair.

Wynette's hair.

She threw it in the trash can, washed her hands in the sink next to her puking companion, and looked at herself in the mirror.

A smile from that dark place deep within her rose to the surface.

CHAPTER 21

"The demon is toying with us," John said as he guided the naked possessed girl down the hallway of the sorority house's third floor. "It's taken hold even stronger than I thought. It shouldn't have been able to break out of the ropes. Did you untie her?" He studied Arnie accusingly.

"No, I swear it. When I came up here, the room was empty and she was in the bath. I thought I saw clear water, and she was all cleaned up inside of it."

"She has her hooks in you." A smile broke out on John's face. "That's good. We can use it."

Arnie wanted to tell the man off. To turn and run down the stairs, leave the house, drop the class, and never come back to Montague College. He just wanted to go home, return to the safety of Raventree Hollow, to be back in the comfort of his grandmother's presence. He couldn't, though. Arnie was one of the few to leave the small town, and everyone would know if he came back a failure. He would spend the rest of his life dodging their ridicule and mocking stares and whispers. He couldn't do that to himself.

And so he stayed.

Arnie followed John into the room and helped tie Melinda back to the bedposts.

"He's hurting me," she cried to Arnie as John secured the ropes.

"Maybe they are a little too tight," Arnie said. He felt bad for the girl whose body had been invaded by a demonic squatter, a tenant whose only mission was to destroy the walls of flesh. Had any part of what she'd said in the bathroom been true? Had she been in his Calculus class, watching as he answered the professor's questions, aced the exams, allowed his neighbors to copy off his paper?

Of course not, you dolt. That was just the demon talking. Turn around and look at yourself in the mirror. He did just that. A tall standing mirror graced one corner of the room. He studied himself, only twenty-two years old and already resigned to a life of solitude. Fleshy without any muscle definition. Pasty skin from lack of sun exposure. Pockmarked cheeks from years of teenage acne. A girl like Melinda would never think of him as anything but the complete disgusting nerd he was and always would be.

He caught her stare in the reflection, her eyes yellow and catlike. A smirk creased her face.

Perhaps John was right. Perhaps the demon really had dug its claws into him. Nothing but trouble could come of that.

Arnie gulped down the dread that filled him like bile.

John turned and studied him after wrapping the sheet around Melinda's naked body. "You okay? I'm going to need you here and present, kid. I figure we have an hour tops before Judith comes back with that gaggle of co-eds, and I want this demon expelled by then. I'd prefer Judith not be here for it."

"Isn't she experienced with this kind of thing?"

John walked to his case on the dresser and reached for one of the books inside. "She gets hurt way too easily. Her ability as a clairvoyant makes her too much of an empath. That, in turn, makes her a liability. The demons like to latch on to her, and it's brutal. There's a connection here already between you and that thing, so that's all we need to keep it distracted while I perform the exorcism."

"So I really am to be the bait?" Arnie asked.

John clicked his tongue. "Now you're getting it. Grab the vial of holy water and let's try this again."

CHAPTER 22

"What is your name, demon?" John asked as he closed his Bible. He'd been reciting a trio of verses repeatedly for what felt to Arnie like twenty minutes. Melinda had just lain there for most of the time, but she seemed to grow uncomfortable during the last couple readings.

"Melinda," she whimpered. "My name is Melinda. Please, just let me go."

"No, demon. What is your name?"

"I already told you."

"In the name of Christ Jesus, tell me your name so I may banish you from this body and send you back to your master in Hell!" John threw a fist down to his side as his words turned to shouts. He looked like a spoiled child to Arnie rather than a professional exorcist.

Melinda lifted her head, finding Arnie standing at the foot of the bed. The uncanny yellow faded from her eyes as he watched, replaced with a sadness and desperation that sent Arnie staggering back a step.

"Please, Arnie," she begged with what felt like sincerity, "make him stop. Take me away from this place. I don't want to be here anymore. I want to go home. He's hurting me." She twisted and contorted in the bed, pulling at the ropes that bound her.

Arnie turned to John. "Should we loosen the ropes? Just a little?"

"Don't be a fool, boy. Give me another cross of water."

Arnie complied, removing the lid from the vial and sprinkling the holy water over Melinda's body in the shape of a cross. It neither sizzled nor caused her to flinch, as if the stuff had lost whatever power it had once held over what afflicted the young lady.

She—or *it*—seemed to notice as well. Melinda's cries turned to the possessor's malicious cackle. "Your magic holds no power over me, holy man," it mocked John.

John slipped the crucifix statuette from his waist-band, having retrieved it from the ceiling after securing Melinda to the bed earlier. "This is no magic, but the anointed word of God."

The laughter grew more cruel. "Different name, same bullshit," it growled at John. "I've watched reli-gions rise and fall with your kind for thousands of years. The wars they've caused. The persecution. The reforming of societies to fit their latest crackpot ideas. I've survived it all."

"If you're so strong, why do you need Melinda's body?" Arnie asked.

"Shut your mouth, boy," John commanded. "You'll

give it more power than it already has. I'll do the talking here."

Arnie ignored him. "Why do you not use your true form instead? You must have a body of your own."

The entity within Melinda shot Arnie a knowing look. "Yes, now you're talking. You know me, child. You know me very well."

"Enough!" John shouted as he slapped Melinda across the cheek with the back of his hand. His wedding ring opened a gash on her right cheek. The girl's whimpers returned.

"Get me away from this monster," she pleaded to Arnie in her own voice. "He'll kill me."

Arnie didn't need to ask her for clarification. She was talking about John Walter, not whatever was consuming her soul from within. He swallowed down his fears, grabbed John's shoulder, and gestured to the door. "Can we talk in the hall?"

They stepped into the corridor and closed the door behind them.

Before Arnie could speak, John pointed an accusatory finger at him. "You're killing us in there, kid. You are giving power to its lies. That's how Satan and his minions work, and you're walking right into their trap."

"I don't think that's a satanic demon in her, John. It's something else."

"It'll say whatever it can to plant doubt in you. That gives it the upper hand. It's controlling you now almost as much as it is her."

"I think you're wrong," Arnie said. He couldn't

believe the words coming out of his mouth. He had never talked to a professor that way. Still, the conviction tugged at his heart. "I know you've encountered a lot of these possessions in your time—"

"You bet your ass I have," John interrupted.

"—but I have seen some things as well. Back home, strange things happened too often to be normal, and I—"

John grabbed Arnie's sweat-soaked sweater vest at the chest. "I do not care about your traumatic childhood and your podunk hometown. If you cannot do what I tell you in that room, then you can go back home and cry to your mommy and daddy and shove off and die. I do not give a rat's ass. I came here to cast the demon out of that idiotic girl, and that's what I am going to do."

John released his grip on Arnie and stormed into the room with a newfound rage.

"This ends now, demon bitch," he growled.

CHAPTER 23

Arnie stood in the doorway and watched as John nearly screamed the words.

"O Lord Jesus Christ, I call for Your mercy to wash over this afflicted woman. I pray for Your blood to wash over her, to cleanse her soul. May it seep through her pores and deep within her insides to the very depths of her inmost being."

"No," Melinda whispered.

"Mighty Healer, I call for You to cast out the demon within this corrupted body. Protect her from the enemy within. Grant her Your salvation, make her white as snow and without the filth that stains her soul."

"No, please," she whimpered.

"My Lord, Defender of Purity, Wielder of the Shield of Faith, I beg You to drive away the corruption in Your daughter and defend her body from further invasion by enemy spirts."

"Make him stop," she pleaded to Arnic.

John sprinkled more of the holy water, this time resulting in the stench of burning flesh as if it had regained its power. "God, I call for Your mercy on this lamb, to spare her from the rod of Satan."

Melinda let out a wet cough. Her lungs rattled. An asthmatic wheeze reverberated.

"May You cleanse the marrow of her bones and restore her temple to how You intended for it to be."

Her legs lifted and slammed down on the mattress, one after the other, repeatedly. Her fingers wrapped around the ropes that held her arms in place, her knuckles turning white at the tight grip. Strings of mucus escaped her mouth as she coughed.

"Something's wrong with her," Arnie cried from the doorway. He took a step toward John, but he didn't know what he could do. He'd already been warned. He didn't want to be thrown out and let the man kill her, so he stood there and remained an observer.

"May Your precious blood wash her clean."

"Arnie," she choked out. "Save me."

He gasped as he noticed how she had turned an inhuman purple. She writhed on the bed, arching her back and lifting her pelvis, causing the sheet to slip upward, bunching up over her chest. Her lower half was revealed once again, but what was between her legs was no longer a shocking sight to the young man. No, it was something else entirely that took the breath out of his lungs.

Melinda's belly had swollen up threefold as if she was pregnant.

John didn't seem to notice. "Drive the enemy out of Your handmaid—"

"John, something is seriously wrong with her," Arnie interrupted, but the man kept going.

"—and breathe into her Your breath of restoration. Lord, in Thy name, we pray for Your child to be free of this evil, of this darkness, of this hook of Satan and his cursed minions. Amen."

The mass in Melinda's stomach moved in odd angles, stretching her skin like a person wriggling under a thin sheet. Her cough caught in her throat.

"Guh." The sound came from deep within her.

Arnie took another step toward her.

"Guh."

He leapt forward and grabbed both of John's shoulders, pulling him away from the bed just as an eruption shot forth from Melinda's mouth.

A stream of tarry black came out like a geyser. It hit the ceiling with force, bouncing off and raining down all across the room, drenching Arnie and John. The older man shook out of Arnie's grasp and darted to his briefcase on the dresser. He threw his Bible in and closed the lid before any more of the strange substance could soak it. Arnie remained where he stood, watching in horror as the flow continued at a steady clip. Gallons of the dark stuff ejected, more than could possibly fit in such a petite person. The smell was somewhere between vomit, rotten eggs, and backed-up sewage simmering in humid summer heat. Death and decay.

And in it, coming from her throat, Arnie was certain he saw something.

Writhing.

Squirming.

Tentacles.

He broke his stare and turned to John to see if the man had witnessed the same thing, but John was diving out of the room and into the hall. Arnie pivoted back. Liquid still ejaculated from Melinda's throat, but it was a clearer mucus now. No flailing tentacles, nothing solid at all. The geyser petered out. A final bit of saliva gurgled in Melinda's mouth, then trickled down her cheeks. Her head went sideways, her right cheek plopped against the soaked pillow. Arnie met her sad, desperate eyes before they closed.

"Is she..." Arnie took a step closer, nearly doing the splits as his foot slipped in the muck all over the floor. He righted himself and moved with more care. Melinda lay there unmoving. "Melinda?"

He reached his right hand toward her face and hovered it just in front of her mouth and nose. No breaths blew out onto his skin. A creak of floorboards in the hall caused him to turn.

"Arnie, look out!" Judith shouted.

Arnie pulled his hand away just as Melinda's head shot toward him, her teeth chomping down on air. For a split second, he thought he saw the razor-sharp fangs of a snake rather than the delicate teeth of the girl, but as she made an animalistic snarl, he realized he'd been wrong.

"What the hell are you doing?" John called from behind his wife in the doorway.

Arnie wiped a slimy string of the dark excrement

from his face. "I thought she was dead. She wasn't breathing."

John waved him off flippantly and pushed past his wife into the room. "I hate to do this, Judith, I really do, but things have gone off the rails. We're going to need you on this next step."

CHAPTER 24

Judith closed her eyes, sighed, and stepped into the room. In an instant, the temperature plummeted. Thick black bile dripped down from the ceiling and froze like polluted icicles over the bed while puddles of the filth froze into slick circles on the floorboards. The humidity on the window hardened. An audible tick came from the glass as cracks spiderwebbed out.

The thing inside Melinda emitted a low growl. Her chest rose and fell with rapid breaths, each exhale marked by a puff of fog. Arnie's undershirt stiffened, the sweat freezing solid. He stepped aside as Judith grabbed the stool from the vanity and sat down on it next to the bed.

"Is she... growing?" Arnie asked. Before his eyes, the once petite body of the college student puffed up with each breath like she was being pumped full of some unseen filler. Her arms and legs ballooned, constricted only where the restraints held firm around her wrists and ankles. The bed looked smaller, Arnie thought, but he quickly realized it was a trick of his eyes. The girl was not only getting thicker, but longer. Her head neared the headboard and her feet dangled over the foot of the bed.

"Not good," John warned. "It's taking form inside of her. If we don't hurry, it'll be too late. Her organs will be destroyed, her bones will snap, and her skin will tear right off."

"You've seen it happen?" Arnie asked in amazement.

John scowled at him and waved a hand toward Melinda. "No, but it's obvious. Just look at her. Of course I haven't seen it happen before. I've never failed at casting out the demon, but then I've always had competent help before."

"Boys, stop," Judith commanded both of them as if Arnie had instigated the man's meanness. He brushed it off.

"What do you need from me?" Arnie asked.

"Step aside, keep quiet, and await further instruction," John ordered. "You'll probably have to hold the girl down when she starts flailing, but until then, don't mess up more than you already have."

Arnie stood there staring, unsure how to respond. John wasn't having it. He pointed to the door. "Stand over there and make sure the other girls don't come in. The last thing we need in here is hysterics."

John studied the second book from his briefcase— a Catholic exorcist's manual—for a few minutes while Judith perched next to Melinda. Judith's hand hovered over the possessed girl's face, shivering from the frigidness. Her eyes were closed and her lips moved, though Arnie could not hear even the faintest hint of whispered prayers or incantations from his place by the door. The cries of the sorority sisters rose up from the ground floor. A part of Arnie wanted to join them, to weep for this poor young woman sprawled out on the bed, filled with something purely evil. He wanted to get away from John and his moods. He wanted to escape what seemed to be an imminently terrible situation. There didn't seem to be a clean way out of this for any of them, but Melinda in particular, especially if John did not acknowledge that the evil inside her may not be quite what he was used to.

"Hit the lights, please, Arnold," Judith said in a near whisper. Arnold did as he was asked. The late afternoon sunlight that filled the room was eerie and distorted through the icy windows, casting the room in a gray tint. Judith's chin fell to her chest as she muttered unclear words to herself, something that may have been Latin, possibly a prayer that she'd memorized from John's book. John's lips moved as well, but the shapes on his lips didn't match his wife's.

A rattle on the floor. Arnie backed into the corner behind the door and stretched his arms out to steady himself against the walls. He'd never been to California, had never experienced earthquakes first hand, but he'd imagined them just like this. The sweat on his palms stuck to the frosted walls, but he didn't care. It took every ounce of willpower not to cry out in fear, but he knew better than to interrupt the couple in this moment or to attract the attention of Melinda and the demon within her.

The bed lifted a few inches off the ground, forcing Judith to stand in order to keep her hand just above the girl's forehead. Melinda grunted deeply, her chest rattling. John stopped reciting the words from his book and watched in as much awe as Arnie. Melinda's stretched and bloated arms yanked at the ropes, legs curling up to pull the ropes taut.

She's going to break loose, Arnie wanted to warn, but it came out as a frightened wail. His left hand drifted down to the doorknob. His fingers wrapped around it despite the biting cold of the brass. He turned his wrist, but the knob didn't budge.

"It's stuck. I can't—" he started to cry out. The bed dropped, its feet slamming onto the hardwood floor. Arnie, John, and Judith snapped out of their trances. The sound caused a couple of the girls downstairs to scream and others to weep louder than before.

"Last warning, boy," John growled.

"Shhh," Judith commanded before addressing the girl. "Melinda, I'm coming inside now. I'll walk you through this. We are going to expel this evil entity from you. Together."

Judith made a droning buzz from her throat. It held for five seconds, and then she spoke in a voice that did not belong to her. "Please hurry," she said. "I don't want to die like this." The voice came from Judith's mouth, but it was clearly Melinda's soft, sweet tone. Arnie caught John's stare in his peripheral vision and reluctantly turned to the man. The smile that formed on

John's face brought him relief. It was working. Judith had made a psychic connection with Melinda.

John held up an index finger in front of his lips to request silence. Arnie nodded and watched as Judith's head snapped up. Her eyes opened wide, but they weren't her eyes at all. They were unmistakably Melinda's eyes. The lids fluttered rapidly. In front of her, Melinda's eyes did the same. Two pairs of the exact same eyes. In unison, both women whispered the same gibberish.

Arnie cocked his head to the side, attempting to pull any familiar words or identify the language that escaped their mouths. Nothing made sense to him. He watched helplessly as drool fell from Judith's mouth, dripping down her chin and neck. A couple feet away from her, a string of crimson blood trailed down Melinda's cheeks, but neither woman moved to wipe away the mess. They remained in their trances, babbling the strange words. In all that was occurring in the room, it shouldn't have bothered Arnie so much, but he couldn't help it. He felt a magnetic draw toward the women. He reached into his pocket and pulled out a handkerchief. Three steps deeper into the room, Arnie turned his head to see if John would stop him, but the man stood there in awe, seemingly unaware that Arnie had moved. The book in his hands angled away as if he'd forgotten it was in his grasp.

Arnie stopped at Judith's side and reached out with the handkerchief. He wiped the string of saliva as it collected in a pool on her shoulder. Her voice cut off in her throat at the touch, and Melinda's halted in unison.

As Arnie took a step back, a darkness like a raincloud overtook the whites of Judith's eyes. The fog swirled within, and Arnie found himself lost in them, unable to look away.

Round and round it went. Arnie's breathing slowed. His own eyes grew heavy, as did his feet.

And then he saw it.

CHAPTER 25

Arnie was no longer in the bedroom of the sorority house. He had been transported somewhere else entirely, some other plane of existence.

The dark clouds he had seen in Judith's eyes now fully surrounded him. They held together like a solid mass, arced in the shape of a tunnel. The ground had give to it, a squishiness that Arnie sunk into. He couldn't turn himself to look behind, but the path forward was dark and unclear. Arnie knew he had to press through it, but every bit of him wanted to snap out of it, to leave this unfamiliar place, to wake up.

He moved forward.

A wet, sticky sound accompanied each step as if he were traipsing through a muddy swamp. Stenches of rotten eggs and wet trash rose to his nostrils, each whiff more foul than the last. Arnie noted an electric buzz in the air. His first thought was that he must be under a network of power lines, but that seemed impossible in this place. As his eyes adjusted to the gloom, shapes took form all around him. Tiny insects, perhaps mosquitos or gnats, swarmed, forming what he had mistaken for fog. Perhaps they were attracted to the rot below him, or perhaps the entire place *was* rotten. Either way, he found he was able to lift his arms and swat at them.

Instead of sending them away, the move caused them to change course. A funnel cloud of the creatures encircled him and swept him up. Grotesque *thwacking* sounds met his ears as he lifted each foot from the gooey ground. He spun like a tornado in three, four, five rotations before the cloud of bugs thinned out. He tripped and belly-flopped into the sludge, pain shooting from his nose as it smashed hard against the ground.

Something brushed against his right thigh. It might have been wet, but he couldn't tell from the sticky moisture that already enveloped him. It was certainly cold, and unmistakably alive. Arnie pushed himself off of his belly, rolling to his side with some effort, strings of stickiness attempting to keep him pinned down. He squinted down toward his legs and gasped.

A serpentine shape slithered only inches away. It was scaly and a sickly grayish green. It twisted and stretched into the hazy distance, with just part of one arc reaching out near Arnie or whatever body he was in. The thing pulsed with life, its muscles constricting and contracting, pushing a thick mass through it, digesting some recent meal, perhaps.

A noise sounded out from somewhere in the distance, muffled by the foul, humid thickness in the air and the clouds of buzzing insects. The serpent stiffened for a moment, then retreated out of view with immense speed. Arnie didn't intend to wait around for it to return. With all his might, he forced his way to his feet and stumbled forward. A shadow loomed ahead, the unmistakable shape of a person. A few more steps forward and the shadow became a silhouette. A little closer and the silhouette became the figure of a woman. A little more still and the figure became Melinda.

"Help me," she pleaded in a small voice. "Please, Arnie. Please help me. I can't do it on my own, but—"

Her voice was replaced by a *gluck* sound. A lump in her throat formed and moved upward, not unlike the mass he'd seen pass through the serpent just moments earlier. She stiffened, stretched upward, then back. Her hands went from clutched fists to fingers stretched outward like claws at her sides.

"*Gluh... hwahh.*"

The sounds cut off as her throat became entirely filled. Just as rapidly, it emptied of its contents.

Those wretched flying insects ejected from between her parted lips. Tens. Hundreds. Thousands. A constant, steady stream flowed out from within her. They were soaked in blood, yet their wings flapped all the same.

Arnie stumbled back a few steps, his hair blowing in the wind caused by their movement as they sped past him. He stood there for what felt like minutes. *There's no way this many of those creatures could have fit inside of her,* he thought, though he knew wherever he was did not exist in the realm of logic.

A plop on the ground drew his attention. He looked down to see a plump worm wriggling at Melinda's feet. Another fell on top of it, then another, until they were raining down by the dozens. He looked to the source—Melinda's mouth—and noted that fewer of the flying creatures were ejecting from her insides, now replaced by the worms.

A thought struck Arnie, though he didn't know why it came to him at that moment. "Where's Judith? Didn't she bring you to this place?"

Melinda could not speak with the parade of oddities using her throat and mouth as their thoroughfare, but she lifted an arm, pointed a finger, gestured behind Arnie. He turned and caught sight of movement on the ground, below the swarms of the airborne insects. From the distance and through the haze of the place, he could not make out the form, but his heart skipped a beat as he thought of Judith Walter dying in this wretched world. If he escaped without her, John would never forgive him.

Arnie stepped toward the low form, swatting bugs as he went.

"Judith?" he called. The sound waves of his voice seemed to peter out just inches from his mouth. He decided talking was futile and may only draw more unwanted creatures, so he ventured the rest of the way in silence.

Movement again, sending another wave of the flying insects away from it. Once they cleared off, he saw what it was.

The serpent.

At least, a small segment of it. The rest of it stretched in either direction into the darkness that surrounded, but from what he could see, this section in front of him contained the lump he had watched working its way through the creature when he first spotted the thing. It wriggled some more within the scaly flesh. Its form took a shape Arnie thought he recognized as the serpent stretched tighter against it, perhaps attempting to crush its bones, smash the life out of the prey it had swallowed whole. It was the shape of a person.

"Judith!"

Arnie dove to the ground and felt around in the muck. His fingers grazed something hard and he pulled it up in front of his face so he could identify it. A piece of bone roughly one foot long, broken on one end and jagged. It would have to do.

Arnie slammed it into the serpent's scales, sharp end first. It punctured through with more ease than he'd anticipated. A shriek of pain rang out in the distance, and the serpent writhed. Somewhere ahead, what he assumed was the front end of the impossibly massive snake monster bolted to its right and circled back. It was undoubtedly moving toward Arnie.

He stayed with the portion that held the mass, moving with it, sawing with the bone shard. Black gooey blood oozed out as he opened the puncture wound larger. Its contents came into view with enough of the flesh carved away. A strand of hair, soaked in blood and slime. A hand, its fingers moving lethargically.

Arnie reached for it and pulled, revealing an arm, a shoulder, a head. It was indeed Judith.

The serpent had moved itself in a full circle before Arnie realized he was trapped. The loop closed in toward him, tighter and tighter by the second, and still he yanked until Judith was free from the beast's innards. She gagged and retched and shot out vomit all over herself and Arnie and the beast. Arnie pushed her away. "Go," he said. "Run."

Judith slid away, the slimy bile that drenched her allowing her to slip over the ground with ease despite the odd shape of her body. *Had her bones been crushed by this snake?* he wondered, but that line of thinking didn't go far before the serpentine beast had wrapped fully around him twice, covering him from feet to chest. It was moving around for one more wrap, which would fully engulf his neck and head. He would be suffocated or snapped in half.

"Damn it, Arnie, wake up!"

The voice came from somewhere distant. It had some reverberation, a quality that didn't seem to fit this strange world. Bright unnatural light blinded him.

"I said snap out of it, you idiot."

The voice. The room. It was John in Melinda's bedroom. Arnie was laid out on the floor in between Judith on the stool and Melinda on the bed. John knelt down by his face, wedged between the wall and the head of the bed. He held an overturned glass that he'd apparently emptied over Arnie to bring him back to consciousness.

"What happened?" Arnie asked as he squeezed his

way back out from between the furniture and stood up. He looked at both women still in the same daze they'd been in before, their eyelids still fluttering in unison.

"What do you mean?" John asked. "Weren't you there? Did you see my wife?"

Arnie nodded. "Yes, but she—"

Judith made a noise that Arnie at first mistook as a growl. As it continued, he realized it was the sound of choking.

"The serpent must be suffocating her," Arnie said. "It must have gotten her after I escaped it."

"Serpent? What are you talking about? Why didn't you bring her back, you useless piece of shit?"

"I was trying before you interrupted it!"

Before the helpless men, Judith was turning blue. John grabbed her shoulders and shook her. "Wake up, damn it. Wake up!"

Laughter rang out behind them, cold and cruel. Melinda. Or, the demon within her.

John lifted his wife from the stool and laid her out on the floor. He pressed his lips into hers, breathed into her mouth, then pulled away and pressed into her chest. The laughter continued to mock them as John repeated the process. Arnie stood and watched. The laughter crescendoed. Maniacal, earsplitting. Something resembling growls mixed with it, interspersed with screams. A flow of tears and blood and pus excreted from Melinda's eyes.

John turned back as he pumped Judith's chest, the panic warping his face into something almost unrecognizable. "Shut up!" he screamed at the possessed girl, then to Arnie. "Shut her up!"

"I..." Arnie reached a hand out and set it on Melinda's right shoulder. He shook her, as if it could wake her from her trance. At his touch, her body rumbled. The whole bed vibrated. The floor and walls rattled. "Something's happening, John. Something's not right."

Cries rose from elsewhere in the house as the sorority sisters panicked from the quaking and the maniacal laughter and screaming and growling.

"What do I do?" Arnie asked, though John could not answer while he continued his attempts to breathe into his wife's mouth and stop her from dying.

Footsteps from the stairwell. The other girls were coming up to check on their friend.

John lifted his head and pumped on Judith's chest. He turned his head toward Arnie and gestured with his chin. "The pillow," he grunted.

"What?" Arnie followed the direction of his chin. Melinda's pillow was slipping off the bed, held in only by a thin flap of the pillowcase.

"Use the pillow, damn it!" John shouted.

"She doesn't need it," Arnie responded in genuine confusion. *Why is he concerned with her comfort in this moment?* he wondered stupidly before realization dawned on him. "You can't be serious."

"Suffocate that bitch right now, Arnold. Do it."

"But—"

"I said *suffocate* her!" John threw an arm out, swiping the stool off its legs and sending it crashing to the ground, rolling into the wall. A startled yelp came from the other side of the closed door. The sorority sisters had reached the third floor. "Do it, you useless slob!"

Arnie yanked the pillow from where it lay and slammed it over Melinda's face.

"I don't want to kill her," Arnie cried. His voice came out childish and whiny, but he didn't care in the moment.

"You'll drive the demon out before it comes to that, and then you can stop," John said. "You'll be saving them both." He gasped for a breath of oxygen, then bent back down to release it into his wife's mouth.

"I'm sorry," Arnie whispered as he put more pressure into the pillow. The laughing continued for a few seconds, muffled by the pillow, but it soon morphed into sounds of panic. Melinda's limbs pulled the ropes taut, then kicked out, then taut again.

The doorknob rattled.

"What's going on in there?" one of the young women inquired. "Can we come in?"

"No!" John called. "For your friend's sake, get back downstairs and keep praying!"

Arnie realized the quaking had faded, but only because it returned in full force.

Items fell from the desk and dresser. John's briefcase crashed down, the vial of holy water shattering on the hardwood floor.

The girls screamed in shock out in the hallway.

The bed rattled and jumped. Melinda's entire body shook most of all, the epicenter of the quake. Still, Arnie held firm with the pillow.

"Kill that bitch," John commanded from his wife's side.

"But—" Arnie began, and then the door opened. The panicked young women glanced into the room, their eyes falling on Arnie. The pillow. Their friend, dying.

John jumped to his feet and lunged toward the door, slamming his body into it, forcing it closed.

And then the shaking stopped.

Judith sat up with a loud gasp for air. John dove back to her side and scooped her into his arms.

Arnie looked down at the pillow for a moment, noticing the stillness underneath it. He lifted it off Melinda's face and tossed it aside.

Lifeless eyes stared past him at nothing in particular.

She was dead.

Arnie jumped back to his feet. "No," he cried. "But you said she'd live through it." He was addressing John, but he couldn't look away from the corpse in front of him. "You said she wouldn't die."

On the other side of the closed door, the girls wailed.

"You did that, kid, not me," was all John replied.

Wynette Strode and the other girls skipped out on classes that Monday. There would be too many questions, too many looks from the other students. Perhaps suspicion was due, but she did not place blame on herself for what happened, nor on her sorority sisters. Sure, she had brought the book into the house, but she had never wanted it read. Sure, Marnie had recommended they use the book to conjure up whatever kind of fun she thought they'd have with it, but she never wanted anyone to get hurt. Yes, Wynette's mother had picked the damn thing out at that estate sale, but the woman never could have imagined it would lead to any of this.

Professor Walter and his wife managed to concoct a story for the police that absolved them and the boy Arnie and any of the girls of suspicion for their roles in what led to Melinda's death. Wynette didn't know how, nor did she want to. All she wanted now was to finish the rest of the semester, no parties or social gatherings or hangouts with her sorority sisters. She wanted to get back home for winter break, to feel Kevin's arms wrapped around her. She wanted to convince her parents to let her transfer somewhere closer to home, even though she was the one that had insisted on being as far away from her family as possible for college in the first place. She just wanted it all behind her.

The day passed with unbelievable slowness. Cries echoed through the halls as each girl came to terms with what had happened. Any time Wynette left her room, she kept her head down to avoid eye contact or conversation with her sisters. She particularly avoided Pam. She was grateful that Marnie had camped out in the social room, allowing each of them to grieve alone. A piece of Wynette wanted to go downstairs to her roommate, who was struggling with guilt for having insisted on using that cursed book, but a greater part of her pushed that idea back into the darkness within.

That night, as with the previous three, Wynette's dreams were filled with the strangest scenes in a dark and foggy world with unearthly creatures and unsettling sounds. Interspersed with that twisted fantasy setting were visions of wandering into the basement, smuggling the ancient book from the puddle of urine, and tucking it behind a series of loose bricks in what had once been a hearth where the furnace now resided. It was a place nobody would ever find. The voice in her head assured her so.

My retribution. My revenge. Melinda was not the vessel I

needed. You are my chosen one, Wynette. Protect the book with your life. When the time is right, I will call on you again.

When Wynette awoke on Tuesday morning, she remembered none of it.

THE TERRORS CONTINUE IN *THE EXORCISM OF Raventree Hollow*.

The exploits of demonologist John Walter and his clairvoyant wife Judith have captured attention around the world. Their tales of performing harrowing exorcisms, hunting demons, and ridding homes of poltergeists are as intriguing as they are outlandish.

Now, they have their eyes set on the small town of Raventree Hollow, long whispered about as a hotspot for otherworldly activity. When they choose the town as the subject of their new documentary film, the community's own local historian and paranormal expert Arnie McCann sets out to expose the couple as charlatans before they reawaken an ancient evil.

Arnie has a dark secret of his own, though, which the Walters threaten to expose if he stands in their way. What measures will Arnie take to protect his reputation—and the entire town of Raventree Hollow?

The Exorcism of Raventree Hollow closes threads from *A More Ancient Evil* and takes readers back to the town from the novel *Raventree Hollow* and the stories "Senior Class," "The Hoarder's House," and "Butterscotch," found in the collection *Ditch of the Damned and Other Tales*. While *A More Ancient Evil* is the only book that needs to be read before *The Exorcism of Raventree Hollow*, the others will also help to paint a richer picture of the town and its history for the reader. All are available now from author Ryan Hoyt and Machete & Quill Press.

Please visit my website MacheteAndQuill.com, where you'll find signed books, ebooks, and more. I like to ship extra goodies such as stickers, coasters, and post-cards with all orders. Buying from me directly helps me retain more of the profit, but I truly appreciate purchases made from any retailer you feel most comfortable buying from.

Please also review on Goodreads, Amazon, and Facebook readers groups to get the word out. Finally, please sign up for my monthly email newsletter on MacheteAndQuill.com so we can stay in touch. Thank you.

ΛΨΧ
LAMBDA
PSI
CHI
Montague College
1966

THE TOWN CRIER

THE NEWS YOU NEED, WHEN YOU NEED IT

A police cruiser sits outside Lambda Psi Chi sorority house where a young woman was found dead on Sunday at Montague College.

WOMAN'S DEATH IN SORORITY SHOCKS COLLEGE TOWN

Police Investigating Sudden Passing of Lambda Psi Chi Student, Age 21

North Abbey, NY

The passing of a Montague College student has rattled the school's Greek Row this weekend. The neighborhood, typically lively with students engaging in intense studying and raucous parties, is a somber site as police investigate the untimely death of who housemates and neighbors describe as a healthy young woman. Police identified the deceased as Lambda Psi Chi member Melinda

THE TOWN CRIER

THE NEWS YOU NEED, WHEN YOU NEED IT

DETAILS SCANT ON MONTAGUE COLLEGE SORORITY DEATH

Police say male student and two professors are not considered persons of interest in investigation

North Abbey, NY

Police continue to investigate the death of Melinda McDonald, a senior from Bangor, Maine and member of sorority Lambda Psi Chi. Witnesses say a male student and two controversial professors of parapsychology were seen at the house where McDonald was found dead, but they are not considered persons of interest at this time. McDonald's family told *The Town Crier* that their daughter suffered from seizures due to a condition diag-

Melinda McDonald, photographed entering a party earlier this month at Montague College

THE TOWN CRIER

THE NEWS YOU NEED, WHEN YOU NEED IT

SUSPICION TURNS TO COLLEGE LECTURER COUPLE PRESENT AT STUDENT'S DEATH

Community uneasy about the pair who teach about the occult at Montague

North Abbey, NY

The campus of Montague College has been flooded with national media outlets this week following the shocking death of student Melinda McDonald. While police have insisted that there is no evidence of foul play, rumors have spread rapidly about the involvement of husband and wife team John and Judith Walter. The pair are lecturers of six courses on parapsychology and related subjects that are considered by many to be pseudoscience, leaving critics

Montague College lecturers John and Judith Walter photographed while traveling abroad in recent years

THE TOWN CRIER

THE NEWS YOU NEED, WHEN YOU NEED IT

OCCULT RITUALS RUMORED IN MONTAGUE COLLEGE DEATH

Police close investigation, but anonymous sources claim there is more to the story

North Abbey, NY

In a shocking update to the story of Montague College senior Melinda McDonald's death, *The Town Crier* has heard claims from a source close to the victim that McDonald and other members of the Lambda Psi Chi sorority may have engaged in satanic rituals in the hours leading up to her death. The North Abbey Police Department issued a statement through a spokesperson claiming no foul play occured, and that they have closed the investigation into McDonald's passing

A recreation of alleged occult items used in the hours leading up to Montague College senior's death.

SAFEA
SATANIST!

This is a novella that almost wasn't. I began work on *The Exorcism of Raventree Hollow* with a twist in mind: the Walters would blackmail Arnie McCann into helping them with their documentary in Raventree Hollow by holding a dark secret over him: that he had been responsible for the death of a young woman a decade earlier. I wrote out a version of the Arnie chapters in this book, intending them to alternate with the "present day" scenes of the novel, eventually revealing the death of Melinda at Arnie's hands halfway through *The Exorcism of Raventree Hollow*.

However, that backstory became so interesting to me that I felt it overshadowed the actual novel's main story. My first thought was to put it all at the beginning and make it one very long prologue, but it was much too lengthy for that. So, a standalone novelette then? Why not. I had already licensed what I felt was the perfect cover for *The Exorcism of Raventree Hollow* from artist Matt Seff Barnes. Then, at the same time I was contemplating making the exorcism sequence into its own standalone work, Matt posted another cover he'd made that was spot-on what I needed, and the composition of the two covers worked perfectly as a duology. Boom!

As I separated the college exorcism chapters, I kept going back to a scene I had written in which John and Judith explain to Arnie how Melinda became possessed. The entire possession sequence came in dialogue where the couple recounted what the other girls in the sorority had told them. There was so much good horror in that dialogue that I knew I had to take it out and actually write out the events as their own scenes. At that point, I came up with the other members of the sorority, including Wynette, and got to inject a little personality into Melinda before she is overtaken by something evil. That brought a more human element to the plot, as well as more scares and a richer story.

After sitting on the manuscript for six months, I touched it up, sent it out to a couple beta readers, and received feedback that the story needed more of Wynette, as it was jarring that she was the point-of-view character in the first half and then not heard from again until the final chapter.

In my final draft before it went to my editor, I expanded Wynette's role and the more subtle possession that overtook her. I am quite proud of the final product, and I hope you enjoyed it as well.

Thank you for reading.

house is far from empty. Something lurks in the depths of depravity.

"Freddy Goodman (Ain't No Good Man)" - He failed his own coming-of-age story. Now he must try again as an adult.

EPIC FANTASY

The Forest of Despair

A heroine's first adventure. A kingdom's last hope. The new female-led epic fantasy series The Pierced Shadow Archive begins here.

The Isle of Abandonment

She once saved a kingdom with her friends. Now she must do it alone. Gemma Calvertson's story continues months after the events of *The Forest of Despair* as she and her friends face their biggest challenges yet.

The Realm Beyond

To help her friends and bring truth to the people of Aepistelle, she must join the ranks of her enemy King Davin and his Royal Mystic Committee. Gemma Calvertson's story ends here.

The Witch of Ferathan

An alluring stranger. A trail of destruction. Will Ferathan survive her charm? *The Witch of Ferathan*, a Pierced Shadow Archive novella, is set seventy years before the events of *The Forest of Despair* and can be read as a standalone story.

ACKNOWLEDGMENTS

Special thank you to my beta readers Stephanie Huddle and Kat Guterman for helping shape the final story. To my editor Amanda DeBord of River Run Editing, I'm grateful for how you cleaned up the final product and helped make it readable. To Matt Seff Barnes, the visual designer of all of my horror book covers so far, thanks for your twisted vision and your dark creativity that bring life and faces to these stories.

Thanks also to my wife, kids, family, and friends for the constant support of my creative endeavors. Thank you to all my readers, to those who champion my books on social media, in Books of Horror and other groups, and give me the encouragement to keep going. To all the reviewers, you help other readers discover new works by adding some stars and a few words about the book, so thank you. Thanks to fellow authors, especially those in the Ghoulish Gains group and the Sacramento chapter of the Horror Writers Association. I'm honored to be your colleague. Even an extreme introvert like me needs camaraderie sometimes.

I can't wait to continue the story of Arnie McCann and the Walters in *The Exorcism of Raventree Hollow*. Stay tuned.

MACHETE & QUILL PRESS
HORROR & FANTASY

9 781956 163230